music
in recreation
and leisure

SECOND EDITION

music
in recreation
and leisure

SECOND EDITION

JOHN M. BATCHELLER
University of New Mexico, Albuquerque

SALLY MONSOUR
Georgia State University, Atlanta

wcb

WM. C. BROWN COMPANY PUBLISHERS
Dubuque, Iowa

Consulting Editor
Frederick W. Westphal
California State University, Sacramento

Copyright © 1972, 1983 by Wm. C. Brown Company Publishers

Library of Congress Catalog Card Number: 82–73286

ISBN 0–697–03561–1

Printed in the United States of America

We call you to join man's race to maturity, to work with us in inventing the future. We believe that a human adventure is just beginning: that mankind has so far been restricted in developing its innovative and creative powers because it was overwhelmed by toil. Now we are free to be as human as we will.

—Ivan D. Illich

contents

preface

This book is a practical guide to the ways and means of planning music programs for both leisure and recreation. It is intended for program directors in the several areas of music in community recreation, camping, industry, senior citizens, correctional institutions, armed services, pleasure cruisers, and clinical settings. In all of these areas, music should have an important place.

The authors believe that all persons connected with recreation or leisure programs should know something about music. This is true of administrators as well as persons actually conducting musical activities. In this regard, it is important to know the bases upon which music assumes importance in the lives of persons from both a social and a psychological point of view. It is also valuable to have descriptions of programs that are in operation and ideas about how such programs were initiated. Finally, it is necessary to know instructional techniques and resources for implementing programs. Helpful hints and practical procedures can often make the difference between a program that functions successfully and one that does not.

This book is organized into an introduction followed by three main parts. The introduction is generally devoted to the need for music in a projected life style. Included in this are the ingredients of a good program. Following the introduction are suggestions for musical activities in various recreational settings. Incorporated into each part is a discussion of the place of music and a general description of program content. Materials are sometimes suggested and model programs reviewed. Finally, the book contains instructional ideas and programs. Here the authors chose to include such related experiences as group singing and song leadership, instrumental accompaniment, sound exploration, choral speaking, and dramatic movement and traditional dancing. In this revised edition the authors have added the program areas: Playing a Small Wind Instrument; Finding, Making and Using Your Own Instruments; and Music and Olympism. There are also many new songs for use throughout recreational programs.

The authors wholeheartedly support the view that music is a source of inspiration through which one can be happily occupied. In other words, music can help to create a positive environment directly related to our well-being. It is with a dedicated awareness of the particular need for music in mankind's continuing and dynamic societal evolution that this book is presented.

The authors also wish to thank Christopher Chavez for his artwork and Karen Webb Hutchinson for her two poems.

introduction

PRELIMINARY IDEAS

The recurrent theme of social change within a "post-industrial" society affirms the need for using our creative energies. From an historical point of view, this need is both crucial and immediate. The change explosion is rapid and only partially predictable. The communication explosion alone is an illustration.

> Imagine a clock face with sixty minutes on it. Let the clock stand for the time men have had access to writing systems. Our clock would thus represent something like 3,000 years, and each minute on our clock fifty years. On this scale, there were no significant media changes until about nine minutes ago. At that time, the printing press came into use in Western culture. About three minutes ago: the telegraph, photograph, and locomotive arrived. Two minutes ago: the telephone, rotary press, motion pictures, automobile, airplane and radio. One minute ago, the talking picture. Television has appeared in the last ten seconds, the computer in the last five, and communications satellites in the last second. The laser beam—perhaps the most potent medium of communication of all—appeared only a fraction of a second ago.[1]

Rapid changes are also reflected in the amount of leisure time we now enjoy. The average wage earner already has 4,000 free hours a year. According to the American Association of Health, Physical Education and Recreation,

> Well over 3,000 communities in the United States spend a total of a billion dollars a year on public recreation to help him fill those hours usefully and enjoyably. As much as 40 billion dollars is spent annually for all types of recreation. Prospects for the future clearly point toward even more leisure and even more income—both public and private—for recreation purposes.[2]

Man's problems relative to the quality of his life style will certainly reflect these rapid alterations in job patterns, work schedules, and income. It was with this in mind that the newly established Institute for Studies of Leisure made its first public statement in 1968 by listing such issues as:

> The human impacts of cybernation, economic and political transformations (such as the guaranteed annual income), a philosophy for abundant time and increasing affluence, classlessness in consuming patterns, extension of significant nonwork commitments, more thrusts of adult education, principles for counseling in the use of new time-bulks, preparation for retirement, and so on.

1. Neil Postman and Charles Weingartner, *Teaching as a Subversive Activity* (New York: Delacorte Press, 1969), p. 10.
2. *Recreation as Your Career*, AAHPER (Washington, D.C.: National Education Association).

The Institute went on to question the nature of new leisure for the middle classes; how leisure is related to the questions of young people; where new values are coming from to meet new conditions of affluence, time, mobility, and mass media.[3]

Such emerging issues will require our best efforts at solving the problems of leisure and recreation. Music and the other arts will, by their nature, supply us with avenues through which these problems may be solved.

Music can be woven into practically every phase of leisure and the quality of life. It is expressive as well as creative. Music affords performing outlets on practically every level and for every occasion. The re-creative benefits of music are numerous. One has only to review the place music could have in the following ranked listing of elements making up the quality of living. These elements and their ranking resulted from a National Conference on the Quality of Life in a Leisure-Centered Society held at La Costa, California in March, 1970.[4] Note that a major portion of the experiences that really count in life are contributed by leisure.

Musical activities can serve as fulfilling agents for each of these qualities. For this reason, the authors have inserted an additional column relating each quality to a musical activity.

Leisure and the Quality of Life

Quality	Musical Activity	Priority Rank Order	Importance (0-100)	Contribution By Leisure (0-100)
Self-respect (Self-confidence, self-understanding)	Solo performance, contribution within a group, ethnic programs	1	100	54
Achievement (Sense of accomplishment, meaningful activity)	Harmonizing by ear, learning to read music, selected for talent shows	2	98	59
Health (Physical well-being, feeling good)	Posture, coordination through movement and dance	3	96	68
Affection (Love, caring, relating, understanding)	Campfire sings, all forms of *group* music making	4	93	61
Freedom (Individuality, spontaneity, unconstrained)	Exploring rhythms and movements, sound exploration and composition	5	91	71
Involvement (Participation, concern)	Group music-making	6	89	63
Challenge (Stimulation, competition, ambition)	Musical shows, competitions, festivals	7	84	56

3. Newsletter of the Institute for Studies of Leisure, Vol. I, No. 1, May, 1969. Inquiries about the work of the Institute may be addressed to Prof. Max Kaplan, Director, Institute for Studies of Leisure, University of South Florida, Tampa, Florida 33620.

4. Report isssued from the Conference on Leisure and the Quality of Life, co-sponsored by the American Association for Health, Physical Education and Recreation (AAHPER) and the American Institute of Planners (AIP). Further information may be obtained from Dr. Donald Hawkins, Consultant in Recreation, AAHPER (1201 16th Street, N.W., Washington, D.C. 20036).

LEISURE AND THE QUALITY OF LIFE

QUALITY	MUSICAL ACTIVITY	PRIORITY RANK ORDER	IMPORTANCE (0-100)	CONTRIBUTION BY LEISURE (0-100)
Security (Peace of mind, stability, lack of conflict)	Group music-making	8	82	51
Comfort (Economic well-being, good things, relaxation)	Listening to music	9	61	50
Status (Prestige, social recognition, positive feedback)	Song leading, harmonizing by ear, talent awards	10	52	37
Novelty (Newness, surprise, variety)	Sound exploration, composition	11	49	50
Dominance (Superiority, power, control, aggression)	Song leadership, musical director, solo performance	12	26	26

ELEMENTS OF A GOOD PROGRAM OF MUSIC IN RECREATION

Elements for a good program reflect the need for enjoyment, self-fulfillment, understanding, and sympathetic leadership. Also needed are informed directors who are aware of the cultural and artistic aspects of living. While pleasure and enjoyment are heavily stressed, this point must not be interpreted as ignoring the acknowledged benefits of quality and depth. A single musical experience is capable of affording great pleasure and enjoyment to those involved. It can, at the same time, be an experience of modest musical proportions. By the same token, persons involved in a profound or complex musical experience may also receive a like share of enjoyment. The intention is to place the stress of recreational music on pleasure and enjoyment first, rather than on an overserious effort to create a perfect production. With these points in mind, selected elements to a good program, equally important might be:

1. All activities offered to any group should produce pleasure.
2. Participants should experience enjoyment and a certain fulfillment of their aesthetic and creative natures.
3. Experiences should be emphasized which are not generally a part of everyday routine.
4. Time should be available in which a person could develop a newly discovered musical outlet.
5. Experiences should be offered that will enable a person to nurture his own aptitudes in various musical ways.
6. Adequate equipment should be available that affords more than make-shift approaches to the creation of an authentic musical climate.
7. Directors, supervisors, and leaders should be aware of the importance of music as an integral part of mankind's need for self-discovery, self-expression, and self-enhancement.
8. Musical experiences should have a direct and positive influence on the immediate environment in which they take place.
9. Excess time and undue pressures should be eliminated so that maximum enjoyment can be maintained.
10. Undesirable and destructive practices designed for technical perfection and performing exploitation must be avoided.

QUALITIES FOR MUSIC LEADERSHIP IN RECREATION PROGRAMS

One imperative for an effective and functioning music recreation program is the music leader who is given the responsibility for its development and implementation. The recreation leader must have the personal qualities and training that are important for all music teachers. In addition he or she should have special competencies that will be valuable in recreational or leisure-time situations. These expectant competencies are listed in Table 1.

DEVELOPMENT OF MUSICAL FEELING AND SENSITIVITY

In essence, music contains many unique characteristics that are often listed as elements, i.e., pitch, duration, texture, color, and form. While not all recreation programs are concerned with developing a high degree of knowledge of these elements, there should always be an attempt to create a sensitive musical environment in which a feeling for these qualities may be experienced. For purposes of clarity and usefulness in the context of this book, the following outline includes an intellectual breakdown of musical elements in descriptive terms.

FEELING FOR. . .	THROUGH	SENSITIVITY TO. . .
1. Rhythm		Beat, accent, tempo, phrase, pattern, silent motion.
2. Linear Movement and Horizontal Line		General shape, direction, phrase, interval, register, rhythm pattern.
3. Quality of Sound		Sound variance, grouping, texture, source.
4. Vertical Textures		Two or more simultaneous rhythmic or melodic lines, relation of harmony to melody, combinations of tonal qualities.
5. Tension and Release		Phrase, climax, dynamics, rubato, texture.
6. Beginning and Ending		Repetition, alteration, change, contrast, pattern, part vs. whole.

TABLE 1

Expected Competencies for Music Teachers and Leaders in Recreation

All Teachers Should Be Able to	In Addition. . . . Music Teachers Should Be Able to	In Addition. . . . Music Leaders in Recreation Should Be Able to
demonstrate a knowledge of physical, emotional, and intellectual development	select the most effective methods for helping each student achieve maximum musical awareness and satisfaction	arrange simple music for various musical combinations
integrate the isolated facts of human development into a substantial framework for influencing behavior	evaluate musical backgrounds, interests, attitudes, and abilities of students	demonstrate the ability to accompany songs and improvise accompaniments on at least one instrument
master the psychological data basic to an understanding of the many facets of human learning	communicate artistic concepts of musical styles and periods	make simple musical instruments
establish an environment which is appropriate to the goals of learners and their needs	demonstrate proficiency regarding the theoretical aspects of a score	create a learning environment that reflects creativity and discovery
radiate a healthy adjustment to the problems of living	perform acceptably on at least one musical instrument	articulate a working knowledge of social elements within a musical group
	conduct clearly and expressively	communicate ideas regarding the role of music in the school and in the culture
	detect and diagnose musical problems in both aural and written form	influence others regarding the unique value of music in human living and inspire them to respond to music in positive ways
		demonstrate flexibility and imagination in meeting new situations

I.
music in recreational settings

The following chapters contain descriptions of eight recreational settings in which music can have an important place. These are: music in community recreation, music in camping, music in industry, music for senior citizens, music in correctional institutions, music in the armed services, music on pleasure cruisers, music in therapeutic settings. Each category of recreation contains a discussion of the role of music and several suggestions for musical activities.

1.

music in community recreation

Music washes away from the soul the dust of everyday life.

Auerbach

Recreation is a vital concern in most communities—both rural and urban. Because of this, municipal governments allot specific funds to support recreation programs. This support ranges from the hiring of trained recreation leaders to the maintenance of community recreation buildings.

Depending upon the size of the community, some type of leadership is definitely required to organize and direct a well-balanced and comprehensive public recreation program. Both the leadership and staff of these programs should be aware of the increasing need for meaningful leisure in society as a whole. They should also know those concepts and ideals relative to the social units they serve. A reciprocal challenge faces the community itself which must lend its firm support to the basic principles of adequate public recreation.

The recreation director will have the ultimate responsibility for initiating ideas relative to the program. He must also see them through in terms of their success. It is hoped that the following guidelines will provide a basis for awareness by those who are directly responsible for planning and maintaining community recreation programs.

1. **An aware director** recognizes that every community has a multitude of cultural resources. One such cultural resource includes persons living in the community who are members of various ethnic groups. These people may be invaluable to the music program by sharing their knowledge of and experience with their own folk music. *Recreational music activities need these resources for enrichment and interest.*

2. **An aware director** includes activities based on the needs and abilities of the people in the community. *Music is a need for all and an interest for many.*

3. **An aware director** knows that a good community recreation program is something far beyond a series of specialized events. *A program without some directed emphasis on music would not be sufficiently broad and well-balanced.*

4. **An aware director** has a healthy, realistic understanding of the importance of worthwhile leisure activities. Not everyone is able to participate in sports in his leisure hours, *but everyone can enjoy music on an individual or group basis.*

5. **An aware director** has the ability to utilize the natural beauty of the community in the recreation program. *Many musical functions are enriched by the beauty of the setting in which they take place.*

6. **An aware director** believes in man's unique creative powers and knows that a recreation program should provide opportunities for a variety of creative experiences. *Music offers all levels of creativity from actual composition to creative listening.*

7. **An aware director** is conscious of music's place in the recreational life of people. *Enlisting the talents of local musicians is one way to augment the music activities of a community recreation program.*

8. **An aware director** has the patience and energy to continually evaluate the existing program to be certain it includes activities for all the young, the old, the average, the slow, the gifted, the spectator, and the doer. *The unique qualities of music allow for its universal appeal in community recreation programs.*

9. **An aware director** knows that a worthwhile community recreation program requires equipment and space. Special effort is therefore needed to locate the appropriate resources for musical activities. These include instruments, books, recording and playback equipment, sheet music, tapes, and scores.

MUSICAL ACTIVITIES AND THE RECREATION CENTER

The musical activities included in a program of community recreation will necessarily vary with the needs of each situation. Rural and urban centers will reflect differences, as will centers located in the midst of ethnic social units. Variance in staff and financial support will also determine the kind of program that becomes an actuality.

Despite these variances, however, most programs reflect the interests and needs of persons who are seeking recreation and refreshment during their leisure hours. The age groups will represent a cross section of both young and old. Human interests and hobbies will conceivably encompass an unimaginable array of sponsored activities. Some of these will come and go according to local interest. Others will remain as a consistent offering throughout the years. In this regard, music generally finds a place of essential importance.

In order to meet the physical needs of a multi-activity program, most communities set aside public space designated as a recreation center ("rec" center). Enclosed buildings are common, together with the adjunct facilities of out-of-door shelters, playgrounds, and parks. Regardless of the facility, it is the quality of the activities themselves that usually determines the success of the program offered to the people. The social nature of music and the multiple expressions through which it is experienced, both formally and informally, make it an especially worthwhile activity within a community recreation setting.

The precise nature and structure of a community program can be as extensive as the imaginations of the directing staff will allow. The following list of activities represents the ideas of many successful recreation leaders. These activities may be expanded according to the unique setting of individual situations. Some may not even apply and should, therefore, be discarded or altered.

GUIDELINES FOR MUSICAL ACTIVITIES IN COMMUNITY RECREATION PROGRAMS

1. Sponsor classes in instrument playing, such as class piano, chord organ, uke, guitar, recorder, etc.
2. Promote community singing programs. These may be in the form of "sing alongs" or community singing ensembles and groups.
3. Institute a "Music Day" as a part of a local fair or festival.
4. Assist in the functions of a community chorus, band, or orchestra.
5. Encourage and sponsor community-wide amateur contests which appeal to all levels of musical talent.

6. Sponsor classes in folk dancing for all age groups.
7. Sponsor out-of-doors park concerts and pageants.
8. Develop a community record loan library.
9. Incorporate music activities and classes into the summer park recreation program.
10. Establish a civic opera which would combine many musical elements.
11. Inaugurate a "Music Week Festival." This could involve all elements of the music program during National Music Week (begins the first Sunday in May).
12. Add "live" music (and musical events) as an adjunct to city skating rink competitions or swimming pool water ballet programs.
13. Plan and present both formal lectures and informal discussion groups dealing with various aspects of music in today's society. People who neither play nor sing are often interested in topics about music.
14. Sponsor teenage dances featuring both local and well-known instrumental groups.
15. Plan activities involving the making of musical instruments. These may be simple in the case of very young children, or elaborate enough to include dulcimers, tub basses, one-stringed fiddles, etc.
16. Sponsor public performances by jug bands, musical saws, etc.
17. Set aside a music room in the center. Included should be music playback equipment for listening (with earphones), and a selection of books and magazines about music.[1] Listening programs may be scheduled and tapes of the center's music programs can be listened to.

ETHNIC FESTIVALS

One of the most popular and meaningful events sponsored by community recreation is an ethnic festival. Exposure to the national character of a group of people often brings with it better knowledge and therefore understanding of our common hopes and aspirations, as well as the distinctive differences among human beings. These festivals have appeal for all age groups. They provide a vehicle for musical folk expression which is always interesting regardless of the level of the talent involved.

Local consulates, residents, and libraries are the primary sources for information relative to an ethnic festival. Newsaper "calls for information" are an excellent way to locate persons who have special talents and information about other cultures and customs. Songs, dances, and recitations usually form the basis for such festivals. Designated dates of significance in the particular culture represented are the most usual times for such festivals to take place. These are most often on the dates of independence.

TEEN CENTERS

A rapidly growing aspect of community recreation, especially in larger cities is the teen center. These are sometimes located in separate facilities or are a part of such programs as boys and girls clubs.

The major emphasis in these centers is personal involvement for social development and aesthetic satisfaction. These goals are achieved with the aid of spirited and enthusiastic leaders who are dedicated to the ideals of current psychological thought.

---

1. See Appendix C for list of *Books about Music for Libraries*, p. 114.

Programs and activities especially suited to these goals are:

Accordion Lessons

Banjo Lessons

Bell Choirs

Boys' Choruses

Combos for Dancing

Folk and Ethnic Music Festivals

Folk Singing

Guitar Lessons

Harmonica Lessons

Jam Session (Rock and Folk)

Jazz Clubs

Jug, Bottle, and Fife Groups

Kazoo Bands

Kitchen Bands

Musical Programs for Shopping Centers

Piano Lessons

Recorder (Tonette) Lessons

Stunt Shows

Talent Shows

Ukulele Lessons

SUGGESTED ASSIGNMENTS AND PROJECTS

1. Check with your local Chamber of Commerce for various ethnic organizations in your community. Discover if any of these organizations celebrate their national holidays and how much music is woven into the fabric of the occasions.

2. Select one dominate ethnic group in your locality and create a program utilizing songs and dances from that culture.

3. Outline how you would organize a musical amateur contest in a municipal outdoor park for a summer evening.

4. List the resource persons in your community who could assist you in developing a city-wide pageant developed around a local theme.

SELECTED REFERENCES

BENGTSSON, ARVID. Environmental Planning for Children's Play. New York: Praeger, 1970.

Community Council of Greater New York. Urban Parks and Recreation: Challenge of the 1970's. New York: Community Council of Greater New York, 1972.

DOELL, CHARLES. Elements of Park and Recreation Administration. Available from National Recreation and Park Administration, Washington, D. C.

EGBERT, MARION. "Music Is What's Happening." Parks and Recreation. (June, 1970):22-24, 57-60.

FARRELL, P. "The Meaning of Recreation Experience in Music as it is Defined by Urban Adults Who Determined Typical Singer Profiles Through Q-Technique." Doctoral dissertation, The Pennsylvania State University, 1972.

FENWICK, P. P. The Recreation Interests of High School Students in Citrus Heights Recreation and Park District, Dept. of Recreation Administration, Sacramento State College, Microfilmed, 1971.

FRIESWYK, SIEBOLT. Mobile and Portable Recreation Facilities in Parks and Recreation. Available from National Recreation and Park Association, Washington, D. C.

GOLD, SEYMOUR M. Urban Recreation Planning. Philadelphia: Lea and Febiger, 1973.

GUGGENHEIMER, ELINOR C. Planning for Parks and Recreation Needs in Urban Areas. New York: Twayne, 1969.

LEDERMANN, ALFRED, and TRACHSEL, ALFRED. Creative Playgrounds and Recreation Centers. Available from National Recreation and Park Association, Washington, D. C.

McCARTY, THEODORE. "Making Music." Parks and Recreation. (April, 1971):25-26, 62-63.

MILBERG, A. Street Games. New York: McGraw-Hill Book Co., 1976.

2.

music in camping

*Join we now as friends, and celebrate the brotherhood
we share. Keep the fires burning and we'll all join in
and sing.*

Summer camps, both public and private, are a firmly established American tradition, and there are thousands of them now in operation. They are generally sponsored by organizations or by individuals who are committed to the life of the outdoors. Some are established for profit-making, while others are organized by service organizations, religious groups, or altruistic individuals.

There are also camps devoted exclusively to the study and performance of music and are naturally patronized by students with musical talent. These resemble a music school or out-of-doors conservatory where music is a serious pursuit and is not considered recreational in the traditional sense. In recreational settings nothing over-planned or tightly scheduled is able to produce the "magic" environment or spell which music is capable of casting over life at camp.

MUSIC LEADERSHIP IN CAMPS

It is generally agreed that it is the campers themselves who should eventually do the music leading. Camp counselors and recreational music leaders should devise programs that will permit this kind of leadership development. The music camp leader's primary duty is to guide and assist. In short, a wise leader "gets out of the picture" as soon as musical events and programs are organized. Here are some characteristics of a good music counselor.

He should:

1. Be a person open to suggestions.
2. Be a person able to follow through on a suggestion so that it becomes a successful experience.
3. Be a person able to recognize and accept a good idea when he hears one.
4. Be a person with an extensive repertoire of songs especially suited for camp life.
5. Be a person with taste and the tact to bring musical events to life without offending or being patronizing.
6. Be a person with an obvious, overt excitement about music.
7. Be a person with resourcefulness in order to utilize limited materials to their best advantages.

8. Be a person with organizational ability in order to organize camp shows, talent evenings, and amateur contests with dispatch and meaning.
9. Be a person able to guide campers in making simple, interesting musical instruments.
10. Be a person with the ability to attract the campers toward a natural acceptance of music as a vital part of camp life.

MUSICAL ACTIVITIES WITHIN THE CAMP PROGRAM

Throughout the day from reveille to taps, many opportunities unfold in which music adds immeasurably to camp enjoyment. Camp life is a self-contained environment and music is ideal in such a setting. The following are occasions on which music can enhance life in camp:

1. *Beginning and Ending the Day.* It is often customary to have some manner of instrumental or vocal salute to the day's beginning. The same is true at the end of the day.
2. *Mealtimes.* A wise leader can inject singing at mealtimes without competing with the physical process of eating. The following illustrate mealtime musical activities: a grace sung before the campers begin eating; a spirited song sung between courses; singing while the campers form a "chow line"; a soloist or small group performs while the others eat; recorded music as a relaxing background during the meal itself; and community singing when the meal is finished.
3. *Campfire Time.* Campfire time is a nostalgic moment in the life of every camper. Songs of sentiment, patriotism, nature, and spirituality can add to the beautiful memories each camper will carry with him throughout his life. An open fire is also an appropriate occasion for persons to perform as soloists. This is also an excellent opportunity for the music counselor to introduce the campers to a new song.
4. *Outdoor Hikes.* There is no better setting for the great songs of the out-of-doors than on a hiking trip. The weary hiker finds strength in singing with others, and the wonders of nature *en route* are given a special flavor by an added song. Rounds and echo songs seem unbelievably beautiful when sung in the hiker's territory.
5. *Spiritual Occasions.* Many camps are under the auspices of various religious denominations. Whether the campers gather in the "Cathedral of the Pines," "The Sabbath Green," or a room designated for spiritual communion, music is ever present. On these occasions the campers' choir of selected voices has an opportunity to share their rehearsed anthem with the others. Here also, is an opportunity for the entire assemblage to sing together.
6. *Just for Fun Around the Piano.* When campers have some free moments it can be expected that one of them will seek a piano in the recreation lodge or mess hall in order to play some familiar song for a group of fellow campers. These informal singing times can be the most popular part of the campers' life. These occasions should be honestly and enthusiastically nurtured by those in charge.
7. *Rest Periods.* Recorded, quiet, instrumental music helps create an atmosphere of relaxation during scheduled rest periods. It may be played through a public address system for the benefit of the entire camp, or on individual tape or disc recorders in various rest areas around the camp.
8. *Talent Shows.* Camp life should be full of occasions in which individuals may express themselves. A musical talent show is a "natural" for this purpose. At these functions campers can sing, play, or dance for the entertainment of the entire camp. Special awards and prizes can be given to campers whose performance captivates the audience. Such recognition and the benefits that derive cannot be overlooked in camp life.

9. *Special Musical Concerts.* One of the great rewards of camp life is sharing in a production requiring many hours of planning, work, and rehearsal. These are special performances which are most successful when correlated with all of the other musical events of the camp. In other words, special events should not absorb all of the musical outlets in a camp to the exclusion of more widespread musical experiences. A well-informed music counselor knows which campers have special talent and the desire to perform. Using these performers and working at specified times during the day, a performance can be presented without undue interference with the regular program. Such performances could include an original operetta or dramatic musical, a concert by a camp band or chorus, and many types of solo performances. Here, too, is an excellent showcase for campers who have been involved with modern dance.

In addition to the above, music offers the world of camping many rewarding opportunities and experiences. An outline of these are given below.

Singing in camp should include:

1. Simple novelty songs
2. Folk songs
3. Nature songs
4. Rounds
5. Serious songs
6. Heritage songs
7. Hymns and spiritual songs
8. Popular songs

Playing in camp should include:

1. Harmonicas
2. Ukuleles
3. Guitars
4. Simple percussion instruments (drums, sticks, woodblocks, etc.)
5. Autoharps
6. Pianos (where practical)
7. Easy-to-carry instruments (trumpet, violin)

Dancing in camp should include:

1. Folk dancing
2. Square dancing
3. Modern interpretive dancing
4. Popular dancing

Listening in camp should include:

1. Recordings of popular music
2. Recordings of serious music
3. Music brought into camp via radio and TV

SUGGESTED ASSIGNMENTS AND PROJECTS

1. Research a collection of 10 innovative and appealing musical ideas which would add to the good fellowship of a campfire gathering.
2. Discover 6 rounds or partner songs of a robust nature that could be used on a hike with a group of teenagers.

3. Construct various original percussion and tone-producing instruments from common materials found in and around a typical camp. Plan a strategy that incorporates these instruments into a musical situation during a day at camp.

4. Using "Nature" as a theme, create a musical production to involve as many campers as possible. Consider group and individual singing, movement, sound effects and meaningful storyline commensurate with the age and type of camper involved.

SELECTED REFERENCES

ALBRIGHT, JOE NED. *The Administration of Summer Music Programs in School Systems in the United States.* Unpublished doctoral dissertation, Columbia University, 1963.

BULTENA, G. L., and KLESSIG, L. L. "Satisfaction in Camping: A Conceptualization and Guide to Social Research," *Journal of Leisure Research,* 1:4:348-354, Autumn 1969.

CHEYETTE, IRVING. *Songs for Camp and Campus.* Westbury, L. I.: Pro Art Publishing Co., 1960.

EGBERT, MARION. "Music Is What's Happening." *Parks and Recreation.* (June, 1970):22-24, 57-60.

GLASHAGEL, JERRY; MICH JOHNSON; and BOB PHIPPS. *Digging In . . . Tools for Value Education in Camping.* New York: National Board of Young Men's Christian Association, 1976. (paperback)

JUBENVILLE, ALAN. *Outdoor Recreation Planning.* Philadelphia: W. B. Saunders Company, 1976.

Music Is Recreation. New York: National Recreation Association, 1961.

3.

music in industry

Despite almost universal belief to the contrary, gratification, ease, comfort, diversion and a state of having achieved all one's goals do not constitute happiness for man. We are coming to a conception of happiness that differs fundamentally from the storybook version.

John W. Gardner

Music in industrial recreation fills many important needs. It serves as a participatory outlet for amateur music-making and also promotes public relations through performance. Several large industrial firms give evidence of first-rate, and even large scale, music programs for their employees.

Beside the requisite of strong management support, the enthusiasm of a good music director is perhaps the most important single factor for success. Several companies report that the ebb and tide of a good program reflects directly on the person in charge of its organization. Company-sponsored music offerings consist chiefly of choruses, bands, orchestras, and folk dance groups. These allow for maximum involvement and seem to be the most popular with employees. Getting such groups started requires optimum organization and planning. In the beginning stages, facilities and equipment are important. The following are recommendations of the National Industrial Recreation Association.

FACILITIES AND EQUIPMENT REQUIREMENTS OF A BEGINNING
EMPLOYEE MUSIC GROUP

The first question often asked when an employee recreation activity is proposed is how much is it going to cost, or what is it going to require in the way of equipment.[1] Below are recommended facilities and equipment for starting and maintaining an employee music group. Not all items are absolutely essential.

1. *Rehearsal Room.* Whether it be a band, orchestra, or chorus, a rehearsal room of some kind is essential. Ideally, it should be a spacious room with good lighting—a room which is acoustically treated, and has controllable temperature for both summer and winter. If the company has no space, perhaps arrangements can be made for one of the music rooms of the public schools, or for space in some other nearby building.

2. *Risers.* Though not necessary at the outset, risers are a desirable goal. For the band or orchestra, the semicircular staging should be about four feet wide, each tier being about six inches above the other. For greatest economy, the risers should be in movable sections so that they can be transported from the rehearsal room to the concert location.

---

1. Taken from *Recreation Management* (March, 1955):27. Used by permission of the National Industrial Recreation Association, Chicago.

3. *Podium.* Whether or not the instrumental and vocal groups are on risers, the conductor must have a podium so that he is raised above the performers and can be seen. A portable platform four feet square that is solidly built is adequate. Of course, podiums can be circular in shape, or made in any design.

4. *Chairs.* The chairs can be of the folding variety and these are widely used. It is best, however, to have chairs that help the performers sit in a good singing posture. Many companies make chairs specifically designed for instrumental and vocal performers.

5. *Music Stands.* Music stands may be either the player's responsibility, or a part of the organization's permanent equipment. The folding stands are adequate, but it is much more satisfactory to have professional stage stands with wide shelves. They are solidly built and can be easily adjusted for good vision. Their appearance, too, is much more pleasing.

6. *Music Files.* It goes without saying that the groups must have sheet music. Building a music library is a gradual and somewhat expensive investment. The expense of music justifies the purchase of files that will make it possible to keep the music in order and in good condition. Sheet music is usually eight and one-half by eleven inches, so that regular office files suffice. Of course, band marches are written so that they may be placed on instrument lyres for marching. If you have a marching band, you will eventually want file drawers to accommodate the smaller sheet music.

7. *Sorting Shelves.* Obviously not an essential item, the sorting rack is an important facility. It is like a bookshelf in appearance with the exception that the shelves are at a music stand angle for the purpose of sorting music for filing or distribution. After a concert, for example, the music must be taken from the individual players and filed. If each selection can be spread out on the rack, the music can quickly be accumulated in proper order. Likewise before a performance, a new selection can be quickly laid out and accumulated for each player's folder.

8. *Mending Machine.* You should have a supply of clear tape for mending tears in the music. There are edging machines available, too, that will enable you to put an edge of plastic tape around the music to protect it from tearing. The machine is not expensive and the music lasts much longer with this kind of protection.

9. *Music Folders.* Each player needs a folder for the music that is currently being rehearsed. Plain manila folders are sufficient. Some music stores have very fine folders available free of charge as a service to local music groups.

10. *Instruments.* Most instruments should be owned by the individual players. It is not unusual, however, that an organization own the Sousaphones, tympani, bass drum, parade drums, and cymbals. In some instances, they may own bassoons, oboes, English horns and French horns. Wherever possible, it's best if the instruments are owned by the players.

11. *Instrument Storage.* Anything as expensive as instruments must be well cared for. They should not only be in cases, but there should be a good storage location where the temperature is even, and they may be safe from fire, water, and theft. Such lockers can be built by anyone who is good at cabinet making.

12. *Uniforms.* Band uniforms, tuxedos for the orchestra, or choir robes should probably be the last item purchased for an employee music group. It is important that the group first prove itself in performance. There is nothing that looks so ridiculous as a beautifully outfitted group that performs badly.

Good uniforms require dust- and moth-proof closeting. If the closet can be lined with cedar and tightly sealed from dust, the uniforms will last much longer. Again a handy company carpenter could build this equipment without much expense.

Music facilities may be as elaborate or as modest as one can afford. It is good economy, however, to provide protection and proper storage facilities for the instruments and wardrobe, since replacement and maintenance costs can be high.

Besides traditional performance in large group ensembles, the recreation program for employees is enriched by such activities as Christmas shows, variety shows, operettas, participation in civic parades, and festivals or pageants. All of these activities provide outlets for every kind of musical taste (from rock to the classics), and for all kinds of musical combinations. For instance, there are barbershop quartets, choraleers, jazz combos, string quartets, drum and bugle corps, and even bagpipers.

Persons of varying ages can participate together. Both athletes and the nonathletes can join in any type of musical activity. But most important of all is the fellowship among employees and administrators in all company departments that usually result from making music.

The following is a partial list of companies and business establishments that have been known for their sponsorship of music programs. Such sponsorship reflects an interest in music on the part of industry.

American Telephone & Telegraph
Argonne National Labs
Battelle Memorial Inst.
Boeing Company
Chase Manhattan Club
Continental Steel Corp.
Dominion Foundries & Steel
R. R. Donnelly's & Sons
Eastman Kodak
Exon
Ford Motor
General Electric
Goodyear Tire & Rubber

S. C. Johnson & Son
Eli Lilly & Co.
Lockheed
McDonald-Douglass
Monsanto Research
Nationwide Insurance
North American Rockwell
Owens-Illinois
Prudential Insurance
Rochester Gas & Electric
Salt River Project
Westinghouse Air Brake Co.
Longines

SUGGESTED ASSIGNMENTS AND PROJECTS

1. Check with local industries to discover if they provide their employees opportunities for involvement with music. If there is a negative response, tabulate some ideas you feel could be included into one of these industries. Make your suggestions economical, practical, and inclusive.

2. Consider yourself the personnel director of a large industry with a budget for employee activities. Devise three ways you would inaugurate music into the employee recreational program.

3. Monitor a class discussion on, "The Arts in Industry: Music."

4. Considering both the cultural and educational benefits inherent in music, conduct a discussion on industry's responsibility to all concerned in this area.

SELECTED REFERENCES

ANDERSON, J. M. *Industrial Recreation*. New York: McGraw-Hill Book Co., Inc., 1955.
EGBERT, MARION. "Music Is What's Happening." *Parks and Recreation*, (June, 1970):22-24, 57-60.
"Employee Music Groups: A Growing Trend." *Recreation Management*, (August, 1969):4-6.
"Facilities and Equipment Requirements of a Beginning Employee Music Group." *Recreation Management*, (March, 1965).
"Industrial Music Is Excellent Use for Employees' New Found Leisure," *Recreation Management*, (October, 1964):10-11.
KRAUS, R. *Recreation and Leisure in Modern Society*. Englewood Cliffs, N. J.: Prentice-Hall, Inc., 1971.
LOPEZ, F. M. *Evaluating Employee Performance*. Chicago: Public Personnel Association, 1968.
"A New Look at Industrial Music." *Recreation Management*, (August, 1964):10-11.

4.

music for senior citizens

Whether seventy or seventeen,
There is in every human heart
The lure of wonder, the undaunted challenge of event,
    and the joy of the game of living.
We are as young as our faith,
As old as our doubt,
As young as our hope,
As old as our despair.

                    Samuel Ellman

Interest in the well-being of senior citizens has risen sharply in the past few years. The retirement years are lengthening and expanding. People are living longer and retiring earlier. Life expectancy is about seventy-three years and will probably continue to increase. In 1940 there were nine million older Americans; in 1976 there were thirty million. More services and programs of all types are needed. Among them should be activities of a recreational nature to enrich the leisure time typical of these retirement years.

Centers are springing up all over the country to provide the necessary leadership for work with senior citizens. These range from local church groups to municipal Golden Age Clubs. There are also senior citizen housing developments of the commercial type. All these groups provide recreational programs.

Much of the impetus for the spread of interest in senior citizens was provided by the first White House Conference on the Aging held in 1961. The conference brought together more than 2500 delegates and produced documents relative to all phases of aging. Among these was the "Report on Free Time Activities" which issued several pertinent recommendations excerpted below.

1. Appropriate agencies should be established at federal, state, and local levels to effect cooperative planning, development, and coordination of services of public and private agencies which pertain to recreation for older people.

2. Emphasis be placed upon the urgent need for education of attitudes at every age toward the importance of active and meaningful use of leisure.

3. Existing public and private areas and facilities be made more available for the leisure activities of the aged; and that the special needs of the aged be considered in the planning and construction of all future private and public areas and facilities for recreation.[1]

---

1. Taken from "Report on Free Time Activities—Recreation, Voluntary Services and Citizenship Participation," Series Number 6, *White House Conference on the Aging* (Washington, D.C.: U.S. Government Printing Office, 1961).

Music naturally becomes a part of every good recreation program for senior citizens. Music has an appeal which can fill many hours of a retired person's life. This is especially true of music which is familiar. The "good old favorites" are always popular among older persons. They enjoy musical activities in which they are actively involved as in piano playing, group lessons on musical instruments, group singing, and various instrumental ensembles. Senior citizens also enjoy listening to music for pleasure and relaxation as well as study. All of these music activities should be voluntary and should never overwhelm persons with little musical background or ability.

As with many other recreational programs, the leader must exemplify a sense of informality and an ability to adjust musical activities to the ability level of the group. In work with senior citizens, the ability levels will be widely varied. Some persons reach their older years having had advanced training in music. Others have had little exposure to any type of music. Musical interests will also be different. Some will be enthusiastic about all kinds of music and will enter into any offering of a musical nature. Others will need encouragement for minimum participation.

Many centers for older people have a music club for those who enjoy listening to serious music. Discussion groups develop from this activity and individuals may even do research in the library on musical topics of their choice. Club members may also present musical activities of a performing nature. For example, the music club of the Guy Mason Adult Recreation Center in Washington, D. C., holds a Senior Citizens Festival every year in May. All senior citizens clubs in the area are invited to participate. Various clubs stage skits, musical numbers, dances, and readings. Participants practice many hours before the performances and render with gusto many musical numbers.

Upon reflection, it can easily be seen that music programs for senior citizens could encompass practically every phase of musical activity. Investigation reveals that the ingredients of success in any music project for older persons is leadership and imagination. The following list of ideas are based upon the experiences of music programs for senior citizens in random communities across the nation. They should help lend support to those wishing to carry on musical activities in their own particular locale.

1. Singing in choral groups is a favorite activity, especially for those who have been church choir or community chorus members and have had to "retire" from this activity due to immobility or confinement.

2. Community singing of an informal type can be successful, provided the leader is capable of producing a relaxed atmosphere. This is especially pleasant on special days, holidays, etc.

3. Group musical instruction on such instruments as piano, organ, or guitar, is an excellent medium for musical involvement. Local music educators are often helpful in planning and teaching. Civic groups or local clubs are sometimes willing to support this activity. These lessons must always be satisfying and should not be so demanding that they frustrate the learner with an overabundance of skills and knowledge too hurriedly presented.

4. Illustrated lectures of a musical nature are sometimes popular, especially in centers where many persons attend local music concerts and events. In larger cities, preconcert lectures about coming musical programs have met with success.

5. Opportunities should be sought by which older persons can themselves contribute to the musical life of their community. Talented persons can often be recruited as volunteers in situations other than those involving senior citizens.

6. Library books about music and musicians are usually of interest to older persons who may, for the first time in many years, have the time to pursue subjects they have always wanted to learn. Music is often one of these. A part of the library collection should also include recordings for listening purposes.

7. The socio-cultural background of the group should be the key to many interesting types of programs and activities. Ethnic music, particularly folk songs and dances will often provide the springboard for many persons to participate. Ethnic heritage tends to take on increasing importance in older years. Cultural roots are aptly reflected in the musical character of a group of people.

8. No single activity should overbalance the program. Individual and group experiences should be in balance as should the nature or the activities themselves.

9. Programs of fun and entertainment should be appropriate to adult behavior which can be entered into with enjoyment while maintaining an older person's sense of dignity.

10. Senior citizens often have hidden or obscured talents. These can be tactfully revealed without embarrassment. Encouragement and opportunity are the key ideas in dealing with talented persons who may be shy or self-conscious.

SUGGESTED ACTIVITIES

The Kitchen Band: One of the most enjoyable ways to make music in an informal way is to organize a "kitchen" band. The numerous interesting sounds one can get from all kinds of pots, pans, and other household items can be explored and used as accompaniments to songs, as sound effects, and even as sound pieces in themselves. Suggested approaches are:

1. Experiment with the sounds that can be produced on simple pots, lids, scrapers, cans, graters, etc.

2. Select a familiar song that has a steady even beat in a moderate tempo such as "Yankee Doodle" (p. 140).

3. Decide on a series of simple patterns that would fit the meter of the song. For example, the following is a suggestion for "Yankee Doodle":

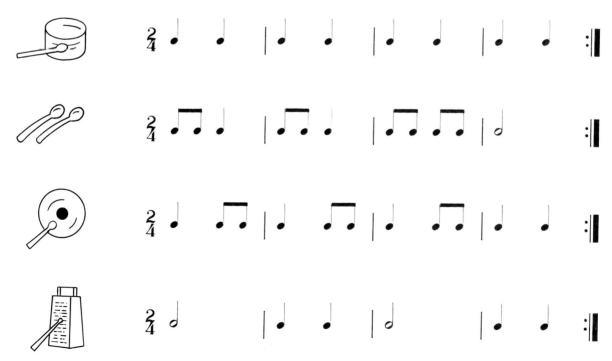

4. Decide who will play the parts. Practice each part separately while singing the song each time. If the players are somewhat experienced at reading patterns, you can play the first pattern, and accumulate the rest in an add-on fashion until all have entered.

5. Record your final performance, and add or change the accompaniment by altering dynamics, changing the pattern on the chorus, etc.

In general, programs for senior citizens in music should also reflect current technological advances. These consist of electronic teaching centers for piano, organ, and guitar. Special instructional materials are provided for group or individual programmed learning on instruments such as these. Technology has now refined the use of transistor equipment, thus enabling persons who want to listen to music to use a compact, portable cassettee tape play-back set with earphones while still enjoying the presence of a group—some of whom may be watching TV, sewing, etc. The future holds the promise of even more convenient and inexpensive ways to enjoy musical activities.

Folk Dancing: Reports are always positive about the response of older people to dancing. Of course, physical ability, stamina, and determination will be primary considerations in this activity, but many people are anxious to become actively involved, and dancing is one of the most satisfying ways of accomplishing this goal. Square dancing, and other simple forms of the folk dance, seem to be the most popular. This is due to the group nature of these dances which does not require a male-female partner as do many social dances. Begin by:

1. Locating a clear, easy-to-follow record with instructions, such as *Modern American Square Dance Series*, Kimbo Records (see Appendix C, p. 172).
2. "Trying out" one of the beginning patterns with one group of volunteers who appear to be especially interested.
3. Showing a larger group your performance and soliciting their membership in your "dance" club.

After you have established a nucleus of dancers, plan a performance outlet as soon as possible giving them somthing to work toward, such as a special holiday get together coming up. Use as many of the initial group to "teach" the others as possible. Be patient with those who move more slowly. They usually improve with the momentum of the dance rhythm and the motivation of the group. Suggestions for many traditional dance steps that can be incorporated into your senior dance classes can be found on pp. 95-98.

Music Listening: Probably the most accessible form of musical enjoyment for senior citizens regardless of their physical condition is listening to recorded music. Even with considerable hearing loss, ear phones and volume controls can, in most cases, enable the pleasures of music to come through the ears. There are as many approaches to listening as our imaginations can afford. Of course, the specifics of guiding a group through a piece will depend on the type and style of the musical selection.[1] The following guidelines may assist in planning this activity:

1. Ask the group for suggestions of pieces to be heard. Their favorites are always a good place to begin.
2. Listen to the music several times and read the accompanying material to gain insight into the music and its composition.
3. Decide on the specific musical ideas you wish to point up to the group or which you want them to discover for themselves.

1. See Appendix B for a Suggested List of Books about Music for Libraries and Recreation Centers.

4. If the piece is descriptive, i.e., tells a story, or describes a scene or event, this will be an important clue as to its enjoyment and appreciation.
5. Before playing the recording, plan an introduction that will focus attention on the music about to be heard. This should not be "dry" or lengthy, but interesting and appealing so far as the specific piece is concerned.
6. Try to plan a way for individuals or the group to respond to aspects of the music. This is especially true of music that has a rhythmic feeling for movement or clapping.

GUIDELINES FOR LISTENING

The following are examples of two listening approaches. The first uses a piece of "program" or descriptive music. The second uses a song with a descriptive text but also calls on the listener to focus on the elements within the music, such as the texture, rhythm, and dynamics.

"WINTER" FROM THE SEASONS BY VIVALDI

1. Discuss the "feelings" and "events" associated with the Winter season.
2. Play a brief introductory section of the composition and discover, through questioning, one or two ideas relating the *sounds in the music* to the ideas that came out of the discussion in #1.
3. Play all the way through and follow the guide below.
4. Listen again and follow the notated themes for each "event."

THE SEASONS by Vivaldi
"Winter"

Allegro	A.	*Shivering* 'mid white mounds of snow *Pierced* by glacial winds, We *run* and *stamp* our feet at every step Our teeth *chatter* with the cold.
Largo	B.	By fire side *quiet* contented days we pass *While* those outside are drenched by *dripping* rain.
Allegro	C.	We *walk* on ice with *careful* pace, We fear to fall, and *watch* our way. *Bravely* we *step*, yet *slip* and *fall*, But we *get up* and *run again*. The ice is beginning to *crack*. *Howling* 'round each bolted door Sirocco, Boreal - - - - winds at war; Such is winter; And it's all worth waiting for!

shuffle shivering

wind's biting breath

run and stamp

chattering teeth

fireside – happy, content

rain outside

ride on ice, walk with care

slippery

slide, step, fall

get up

ice should crack

hear . . . .

winds at war . . . .

"This Old Guitar" by John Denver
(recording: *Back Home Again*)

The list below describes the feelings John Denver has about his guitar. Listen. Can you add any more words or phrases to this list?

FRIENDSHIP: LOVE; WAY OF SHARING HIS MUSIC;

Listen again and check the musical ideas you heard in the song. Can you add others you heard?

1. ☐ ONE MELODY WITH ACCOMPANIMENT
2. ☐ SEVERAL MELODIES TOGETHER

1. ☐ STEADY METER
2. ☐ UNSTEADY METER

1. ☐ MANY DYNAMIC CHANGES
2. ☐ FEW DYNAMIC CHANGES

Now, relax and listen to the music. Feel the mood created by the overall flow of the guitar part and the voice part. Listen to other songs of John Denver's. Which are your favorites? Why?

Somehow, the leisure time of the older years must be filled with positive, enriching experiences if we are to maintain the credibility of a nation growing in civilized and cultural awareness.

SUGGESTED ASSIGNMENTS AND PROJECTS

1. Organize a musical program appropriate for active senior citizens. How can music serve the inactive senior citizen?
2. List the resource persons in your community who would be available to enrich the musical aspects of a recreational program for senior citizens.
3. Create a bulletin board for a senior citizen headquarters giving information about the musical events in the center for a given month.
4. Visit a local Senior Citizen Center and discover how music is used in its over-all program.
5. Volunteer to arrange an evening of music for a local Senior Citizen Center.
6. Outline ways a young recreation director can identify with music of the senior citizen in order to provide the kinds of musical events commensurate with this group.

SELECTED REFERENCES

Carlson, Adelle. *Songs to See and Sing*. Nashville, Tenn.: Broadman Press, 1971.
Carnegie, Dorothy. *Don't Grow Old—Grow Up*. New York: E. P. Dutton and Co., Inc., 1959.
Davidson, Jessica. "Music and Gerontology." *Music Educators Journal*. (May, 1980):27-31.
Gill, H. "Music in Recreation Programs for Senior Citizens," Department of Recreation and Park Administration, Clemson University, 1973.
Harris, L., and Assoc., Inc. *The Myth and Reality of Aging in America*. Washington: National Council on Aging, January, 1976.
Hedges, Sid G. *Fun for the Not So Young*. New York: Philosophical Library, n.d.
Institute of Lifetime Learning. Box 292, Long Beach, California 90801.
Johnson, Alton C., and Prieve, Arthur. *Older Americans: The Unrealized Audience for Arts*. Madison, Wis.: Center for Arts Administration, 1975.

KLEEMEIER, ROBERT W. *Aging and Leisure*. New York: Oxford University Press, 1961.

MADOW, PAULINE. *Recreation in America*. New York: H. W. Wilson Co., 1965.

MATHIASEN, GENEVA. *Criteria for Retirement*. New York: Putnam's Sons, n.d.

MERRILL, M. A. *Social Clubs for the Aging*. Springfield, Ill.: Charles C Thomas, Pub., 1973.

MULAC, MARGARET. *Leisure-Time for Living and Retirement*. New York: Harper and Brothers, 1961.

Myth and Reality on Aging in America. Washington, D. C.: National Council on the Aging, 1975.

Recreation for Later Maturity, March 1956 Bulletin No. 18, North Carolina Recreation Commission, 1956.

Recreation for Older Adults, by Adelle Carlson. Church Recreation Service, Baptist Sunday School Board, Nashville, Tenn., n.d.

Recreation for Senior Citizens, A Report of the Third Southern Regional Institute on Recreation for the Aging. "Retirement—A New Way of Life," by Eugene Friedman, Ph.D., University Extension Division, University of Wisconsin, Madison, Wis.

SALMON, IRVIN. *Retire and Be Happy*. New York: Greenberg Pub., n.d.

SMARIDGE, N. *Choosing Your Retirement Hobby*. New York: Dodd Mead and Co., 1976.

STAFFORD, VIRGINIA, and EISENBURG, LARRY. *Fun for Older Adults*. Nashville, Tenn., Parthenon Press, 1956.

SUNDERLAND, J. T. *Older Americans and the Arts: A Human Equation*. Washington, D. C.: National Council on Aging, 1974.

WEINSTOCK, HERBERT. *What Music Is*. New York: Doubleday, 1953 and 66.

5.

music in correctional institutions

He drew a circle that shut me out,
Heretic, rebel, A thing to flout;
But love and I had wit to win,
We drew a circle that took him in.
Edwin Markham

In modern, enlightened institutions, music has beeen justified as a rehabilitating agent and also as entertainment. This reflects an attitude on the part of prison officials who are looking for new ways to effect behavior changes. In this context, a comprehensive view of recreation which includes music is receiving increasing attention. Evidence of this is appearing in the literature on correction. One illustration is the following statement taken from the latest edition of the well-known book, *The Sociology of Punishment and Correction* by Johnston, Savitz, and Wolfgang: "Early prison reformers hoped that unpleasantness, hard work, solitude, and education would reform men. Contemporary penologists, however, are increasingly aware how difficult it is to affect permanent changes . . . within a prison setting, and . . . are more willing to experiment with new techniques."[1] The authors go on to suggest group and social activities. Music could be a part of many of these.

Music involves many facets of group and individual response. When specifically applied to the needs of persons under correction, these responses can be very positive. The following is a partial list of benefits to be derived from musical participation.

1. Can be effective in evoking interest for some inmates when other means fail.
2. Offers relief from the feelings of confinement.
3. Can become a nonverbal means for anxiety reduction and the release of frustration.
4. Group music-making can provide a sense of belonging and help to alleviate feelings of isolation.
5. Can fill many dull hours, especially for persons with long sentences.
6. Help to reduce feelings of listlessness that sometimes result from serving time.
7. Practice and achievement in instrument playing helps to build morale and self-worth in the accomplishment of a task that continues in difficulty as well as satisfaction.

1. Norman Johnston, Leonard Savitz, and Marvin Wolfgang, *The Sociology of Punishment and Correction* (New York: John Wiley, 1970), p. 497.

The character and expressive power of music enable persons of all ages and backgrounds to derive value from either listening or being actively involved in music-making experiences. Music consists of a wide variety of styles—from hillbilly to the classics. It can also be experienced in diverse ways, ranging from simple folk guitar playing to orchestral performance.

Many large correctional institutions have incorporated musical activities into their recreational programs. In a 1965 survey of twenty prisons, nine had bands, seven had orchestras, and six had choirs or glee clubs. All of the prisons reported musical activities and events on special days or as a part of religious services. While trained recreational directors were hired by all institutions, ten had full or part-time professionals in music. In several instances, prisons allowed talented and trained inmates to guide or direct musical events. These were generally reported to be superbly handled, especially on the part of instrumentalists who were often skilled performers upon prison entrance.[2]

Therapeutic arts programs for prisoners have also been supported by the Expansion Arts Program of the National Endowment for the Arts and by a million-dollar grant from the Law Enforcement Assistance Administration. According to the panel report chaired by David Rockefeller, Jr. entitled *Coming To Our Senses*, the above programs support professionally directed arts projects inside prisons as well as community-based correction programs combining ethnic folk arts traditions as well as vocational skills as a result of apprenticeships with professionals.[3]

In addition to hired professionals and inmates, many correctional institutions encourage talent from outside the institution. This usually functions as entertainment and is a welcome source of recreation for many inmates. The planning and scheduling of such events is a major responsibility of the recreation director. The following guidelines may help in terms of organization.

1. Musical events should reflect a variety of types and styles.
2. Events should be well publicized among the entire institutional population. A special point should be made to inform those who have special interests or skills related to the coming event.
3. Music events should reflect the totality of psychological experience including the dramatic and sentimental as well as the humorous and heroic.
4. Musical events should not be scheduled when sports activities would be in conflict.
5. Provide visiting performers with suggestions based upon past successful programs.
6. Record performances for use at later times.

It must be emphasized that the problems and institutional needs relative to correction are complex and multiple. There are many types of institutions ranging from juvenile training centers to federal prisons. In this regard, generalizations are difficult to make. In some instances a music program of an educational type can be of value in rehabilitation. In other instances music will consist chiefly of entertainment during recreation periods only. According to the American Correctional Association, the ideal attempt is to establish a balanced program of work, training, and recreation in the day-to-day life of a correctional institution. Based on this view, music can become a reward and reinforcement for work and training.

2. Student Research Team, George Waldie, Chairman, Departments of Recreation and Music, University of New Mexico, 1965.
3. *Coming To Our Senses*. Arts, Education and Americans Panel. New York: McGraw-Hill Book Company, 1977, pp. 178-180.

Music can also stand alone as a constructive source for rehabilitation. It can become a means for use of leisure and recreation. In many training centers for young people, for example, musical events (and even instruction) take on the aspects of typical school music programs in public schools. Supervised athletics, plays, pageants, folk dancing, and musical festivals are among the sponsored events in such institutions.

Regardless of the setting in which it becomes a part, music will serve many valuable functions of institutional correction. In general it can help to bridge many difficulties that arise from confinement and isolation.

SUGGESTED ASSIGNMENTS AND PROJECTS

1. Prepare a meaningful questionnaire directed to prison authorities seeking their opinions regarding music's worth in their programs.

2. Write a short paragraph explaining how you would go about seeking and organizing the musical talent present in a correctional institution. Discuss this paragraph with others in your class.

3. List unique, musical activities that could be offered to meet the challenge of correctional environments.

4. Research the value that participation in the Arts (Music) has for persons in a correctional setting and present this data to your class to stimulate group discussion.

SELECTED REFERENCES

American Correctional Association. *Proceedings, 1969 Annual Congress of Correctional Associations.* Washington, D. C.: ACA, 1970.

JOHNSTON, NORMAN; SAVITZ, LEONARD; and WOLFGANG, MARVIN. 2nd ed., *The Sociology of Punishment and Correction.* New York: John Wilry, 1970.

ROSSMAN, PARKER. "Appropriate Punishment: The Key to Rehabilitating Criminals," *The Futurist,* (April, 1981):41-47.

6.

music in the armed services

*The bow cannot possibly always stand bent, nor can human
nature or human frailty subsist without some recreation.*
Cervantes

Musical activities can be among the richest offerings of any recreational program for the armed services. All soldiers can participate as either listeners or performers. For example, during one year at Fort Sam Houston, the attendance for the Fourth Army Entertainment Program alone was 772,121. This would be doubled with the inclusion of service club musical and entertainment activities.[1]

To illustrate the widespread nature of music related activities, one has only to read the Army regulation for the administration of facilities and personnel assigned to entertainment-related programs. The text of this regulation follows.

Section I. General

1. *Mission.* The mission of the Army entertainment program is to assist in developing the efficiency and morale of military personnel through cultural, vocational, avocational, creative and/or recreational pursuits by planning, promoting, and developing theatrical and musical activities as an effective means of providing adult special interest outlets in all phases of the performing and tributary arts.

2. *Scope.* The Army entertainment program includes within its functional scope three subprograms of activity: music, theater, and touring shows. Each subprogram is of equal importance in the accomplishment of the mission of the program, is closely allied, and generally interrelated in the development of the overall program. Figures 1, 2, and 3 indicate the sources of touring shows and the activities of the music and theater programs.

   a. Touring shows. Live (professional or amateur, civilian or military, theatrical or musical attractions produced elsewhere and brought to an installation to perform in facilities other than clubs and messes.

   b. Music. All organized music including vocal, instrumental, technical, and listening music activities, except authorized TOE Army bands.

      (1) Vocal activities. Activities which include individual and group recital and concert forms; individual and group folk, popular, country and western, jazz, patriotic and/or military, religious, semiclassical, and classical forms, as well as other types of choral and ensembles (singing in unison or in harmonic parts), both large and small including quintets, quartets, trios, and duos, contests and festivals; choral

---

1. Taken from a returned questionnaire completed by the Staff Service Club Director, Fort Sam Houston, Texas, 1968.

workshops and/or clinics; singing platoons, singing-on-the-march, and song fests of all types. Solo and group forms may include instrumental accompaniment or be performed a capella, as appropriate.

(2) Instrumental activities. Activities which include the development, maintenance, and use of show and dance bands; small instrumental combinations; individuals and groups specifically developed for use in musical theater activities; individual and group recital and concert forms; individual and group popular, country and western, rhythm and blues, rock and roll, jazz, dixieland, semiclassical, and classical forms; musical ensembles of all types; symphonic, orchestral, chamber, and band groups, as well as all types of solo performances; contests and festivals; solo and group practice sessions; music fairs, and music workshops and clinics.

(3) Technical music activities. Activities which include musical direction; composition and/or creative writing; theory and harmony; arranging and orchestration; music copying; music management; interpretation of musical styles; lyric writing; accoustics; rehearsal and performance techniques of all types; and care and maintenance of all types of musical equipment.

(4) Listening activities. A series of carefully planned and produced listening programs including all types of recorded music; live performances by musical artists (both vocal and instrumental), lecturers, critics, and teachers; music education and appreciation activities; demonstrations and clinics by all types of musical and educational organizations and/or individuals. Emphasis is placed on carefully annotated programs emphasizing high performance standards whether program is performed live or recorded.

c. Theater. All organized theatrical activity including dramatic musical-theater, technical, and listening programs.

(1) Dramatic activities. Activities which encourage the development of spoken art forms to include plays of all types (tragedy, comedy, farce, melodrama, and all other types); individual dramatic readings and/or monologs; sketches, skits, and blackouts; large and small dramatic groups; play-reading groups; choral speech or reading groups; little theater groups; dramatic workshops and clinics; drama contests and festivals; radio and television workshops and productions.

(2) Musical-theater activities. Activities which include musical comedies, musical dramas, musical revues, operas, operettas, thematic productions of all types; variety shows; band shows; dance productions of all types; contests and festivals; all other forms of musical theater whether performed individually or by a group.

(3) Technical theater activities. Activities which include theatrical directions; playwriting; and other forms of creative writing; lighting design and implementation; scenic and costume design and construction; makeup; stage management; oral interpretation, play production; choreography; dance production; techniques of announcing; technical production; sound reproduction; rehearsal and performance techniques of all types; and care and maintenance of all types of theatrical equipment.

(4) Listening activities. A series of carefully planned and produced listening programs including all forms of theatrical materials; live performances by theatrical artists, lecturers, critics, and teachers; demonstrations and clinics by all types of theatrical

and educational organizations and/or individuals. Emphasis is placed on carefully annotated programs emphasizing high performance standards whether a program is performed live or recorded.[2]

As a morale factor, music has been recognized since the Fife and Bugle Corps during the Revolutionary War. The military band has been integral to the armed forces since the Civil War and singing was widely encouraged during the First World War—as witnessed by the many well-loved songs of that period.

Recreation specialists in music with the Armed Forces Special Services often come from the ranks of career employees. Aside from their status, however, these specialists are required to have the Baccalaureate Degree in vocal or instrumental music plus two years of successful teaching experience directing a variety of musical activities. Experience as an entertainer or performer is non-qualifying.

The day-to-day work of service music personnel can be highly creative. Special Services officers and club directors are constantly challenged to find imaginative ways involving service men in musical groups and performances. Variety shows are among the most popular ways. Most service clubs schedule these regularly. The following schedule is typical. The music and dance events are underlined.

MAY 1970

SUNDAY	MONDAY	TUESDAY	WEDNESDAY	THURSDAY	FRIDAY	SATURDAY
1000 Morning Music 1300 Jam Session 1500 Ping Pong Contest 2000 Soldier Show						1000 Record Requests 1300 Art Corner 1900 May Bingo 1915 The Whitman Dancers Show
1000 Morning Music 1300 Combo Time 2000 Soldiers Entertain	1900 Ceramics Class 2000 Leathercraft Class	1900 Classical Record Requests 2000 "May" Dance	1900 Classical Record Requests 2000 Gameroom Contests	1900 "Life and Yahtze" Games 2000 Movies Refreshments	2030 "Pioneer" Dance	1000 Record Requests 1300 Art Corner 1500 Bridge Games 1900 Record Roulette 2045 Soldier Show
1000 Morning Music 1300 Club Combo 2000 Soldier Show	1900 Ceramics Class 2000 Leathercraft Class	1900 Classical Record Requests 2000 "Spring is Here" Dance	1900 Pokend Games 2000 Pool, Ping Pong Contests	1900 Concentration 2000 Movies Refreshments	1900 Chuck-a-luck Games 2000 "You can Use It" Bingo	1000 Record Request 1300 Art Corner 1500 Bridge Games 1900 Combo Rehearsal 1915 Starlit Revue Show

Continued on page 28.

2. Issued by U.S. Army, Regulation AR 28-13, TAGO 7841.

MAY 1970

SUNDAY	MONDAY	TUESDAY	WEDNESDAY	THURSDAY	FRIDAY	SATURDAY
1000 Morning Music 1300 Guitars and Songs 2000 Visiting Combo	1900 Ceramics Class 2000 Leathercraft Class	1900 Dance Class 2000 "Ballroom" Dance	1900 Soldier Birthday Party 2000 Gameroom Contests	1900 Two for the Money	1900 Company Team Party 2000 "Consequence" Bingo	1000 Record Request 1300 Art Corner 1900 Game-a-rama 2045 Dorothy Inderleid Show
1000 Morning Music 1300 Jam Session 2000 Soldiers Entertain	1900 Ceramics Class 2000 Leathercraft Class	1900 Classical Music Requests 2000 "Spring" Dance	1900 Horse Race Games 2000 Pool, Ping Pong Contests	1900 Bowling 2000 Movies Refreshments	1900 Video Village Game 2000 "Smokers" Bingos	1000 Record Request 1300 Art Corner 1915 Belmont Fun

SUGGESTED ASSIGNMENTS AND PROJECTS

1. Visit a local recruiting office and interview the commanding officer regarding recreational activities in their branch of the service.

2. Tour a service camp in your area and outline the arts and recreational activities planned for a 2-week period. Also, interview the agency or officer in charge of recreational activities.

3. Observe a rehearsal or performance of a service performing organization such as a band or chorus in your area. Discuss the performing options with the director of the group.

4. Compile a survey of local veterans and ask questions regarding how they felt their entertainment needs were met when they were in service.

7.

music on pleasure cruisers

This much I know when all is done,
That he who's never tasted fun
Will think of life as one grand bore
And shouldn't get to Heaven's door.
John Batcheller

Recreation work aboard ship is probably the most glamorous in the field. It is associated with travel, new sights, interesting people, and the attendant excitement of visiting foreign ports. Because of this, positions for qualified directors or social leaders may be limited. However, there appears to be a signal that this situation may change. According to a December, 1981 NBC news report, there is a 30% rise in cruise travel. Predictions are that this will continue as people look for new vacation alternatives.

Qualification requirements always include previous experience in resorts, country clubs, or hotels. In addition, most ship lines have such requirements as the ability to speak at least one foreign language, some knowledge of ports to be visited, organizational ability, and most important of all, a pleasant personality with which to confront various situations and many different kinds of people.

On the larger cruise vessels, music permeates most recreational activities, either as a direct participative experience or as a background for an event. Orchestras and dance bands are probably the most common form of musical entertainment. Roving musicians with solo instruments, such as accordion or violin, are becoming more popular. Recorded music is piped into staterooms, and onto game decks and pool areas. Active music participation in passenger choruses and talent shows are effective leisure activities common on mainline cruises.

Additional facilities in which music could have a part include a 10,000 book libary on the S. S. France, a 66,000 ton vessel carrying 2044 passengers. A selection of recordings and tapes with earphones could be added to such a ship library. Books about the lives of musicians or the art of music would naturally be of interest to many passengers. For many people, the relaxing atmosphere of cruise travel provides a first opportunity to "take the time" to explore the arts. Busy work routines and the pressure of responsible jobs are left on shore. The leisure time away from the telephone can be filled with rewarding pleasures always thought too time consuming at home.

The theater, used primarily for movies, is also available for talent shows and music productions on board the larger vessels. For example, the MS Sagafjord, on the Norwegian-American Line (21,000 tons) has a 250 seat theater that is used for numerous events and musical programs including travel talks about each port of call. These talks might include local onshore musical events, concerts, and folk festivals which passengers might attend. Such musical events often become memorable highlights of travel cruises and form the basis for cultural understanding.

On many pleasure cruisers, music permeates the events of each day. The following schedule is typical. The several events which include music or related activities are in bold.

EVENTS DU JOUR

7:00 A.M.	Breakfast is served		4:15 P.M.	**Recorded concert**
8:00 A.M.	Holy Mass		4:30 P.M.	Clay pigeon shooting
8:00 A.M.	Calisthenics		4:30 P.M.	Register for children's costume party
9:00 A.M.	Protestant services			
10:00 A.M.	Holy Mass		5:00 P.M.	Children's costume party
10:00 A.M.	Your lesson in French		6:15 P.M.	Your late news report
10:30 A.M.	Hostess hour		6:30 P.M.	Cocktails are served in all bars
11:00 A.M.	**Free dance lesson**			**(Music in Riviera Lounge and Left Bank Cafe)**
11:00 A.M.	**Teen-age fun and games**			
11:00 A.M.	Clay pigeon shooting		7:30 P.M.	Dinner is served
11:30 A.M.	Your morning forum at sea		9:00 P.M.	**Dance music**
11:45 A.M.	Aperitif time (Music in the Riviera Lounge)		9:30 P.M.	**Music for dancing**
			10:00 P.M.	**Ball Apache**
12:30 P.M.	Luncheon is served		10:00 P.M.	Young adults swimming party
12:30 P.M.	Buffet luncheon is served		TO	
TO			MIDNIGHT	
2:00 P.M.			10:30 P.M.	"Surprise a la Francaise"
2:30 P.M.	Duplicate bridge tournament		11:00 P.M.	Noctambules (night owls)
3:00 P.M.	Informal card games		11:00 P.M.	**Music by Alicia John Trio**
3:30 P.M.	Shuffleboard tournament begins		MIDNIGHT	**Piano magic**
4:00 P.M.	Need help with your Apache costume		MIDNIGHT	Buffet is served
4:00 P.M.	**Tea and bingo (music in the St. Tropez Lounge)**		TO 1:30 A.M.	

There are numerous steamship and pleasure cruise lines. Each has special activities for passengers according to number of persons aboard, size of ship, ports of call, time of year, etc. Upon inquiry, it was reported that the smaller transport ships, carrying as few as twelve passengers obviously have no recreation director as such. However, recreational facilities are almost always available.

SUGGESTED ASSIGNMENTS AND PROJECTS

1. Interview a local travel agency about the recreational opportunities onboard cruise ships with which they are familiar. Obtain literature and determine the extent of these opportunities in their advertisements.

2. Plan your own calendar of activities for a 5-day cruise which would include a variety to meet various needs and age groups.

3. Interview a local person who has recently been on a cruise ship. What were the impressions regarding recreational activities?

8.

music in therapeutic settings

*Man is, properly speaking, based upon hope; he has no
other possession but hope; this world of his is emphatically
the place of hope.*

Carlyle

The entire field of Music Therapy is vast and highly specialized. For this reason it is impossible to include a comprehensive program here. However, there are several theoretical and practical suggestions for treatment which could provide an introduction to the field in general. Anyone interested in specializing in Music Therapy should be prepared to receive considerable training. Primary in this training should be a background in music methods—both general and specific.

Music Therapy is the use of music in the education and the treatment of persons needing special help resulting from functional disorders. It is directly involved with both rehabilitation and education. Used therapeutically, music releases anxieties. Even the smallest accomplishments in mastering a musical activity will build confidence and self-worth. It is expressive and does not require words. Thus music provides a natural means for expressing feelings and moods. Music stimulates the individual as a whole and creates an environment that is noncompetitive and undemanding. It is also appealing and stimulates response.

In addition, musical problems may be approached through the development of skills and concepts. These are essential to the nature of music in terms of its elements, i.e., pitch duration, texture, color, form. These are likewise the results of experiences in listening, singing, playing instruments, moving to music and creating music. Authentic responses of this type can be made in therapeutic settings, regardless of the level of responses or the quality of the rendition.

Music can help to solve problems for many persons with emotional or mental disorders. Generally, their problems include tension, fear, depression, defensiveness, and disorganization in thought patterns as well as problems which are the result of physical impairment. Consequently these persons need communication, interaction with others, confidence, and a sense of belonging. They also need to discover avenues which can lead them toward better physical coordination and ways of making legitimate compensations.

For the recreational leader involved in therapeutic music the following are some musical assets which may serve as guidelines.

That music:

1. Can establish communication without verbalization and can also serve to stimulate verbalization when needed.

2. Eliminates the friction which words may produce.
3. Overcomes antagonism, isolation, and nonparticipation.
4. Attracts attention, produces various moods, and stimulates imagery.
5. Offers a variety of skill levels. A person with a low failure factor can experience a feeling of achievement as he masters a simple musical response, such as striking a triangle, beating a drum, or simply tapping his foot.
6. Affords a variety of expressive outlets. For example, emotions can be expressed musically by uncomplicated listening experiences. In this instance, a person is not required to perform any kind of physical act that might otherwise prove threatening. Improvisation on an instrument often allows emotions to be released, or even, in some instances, discovered. The many ways a person can move himself or parts of his body to music can be another expressive outlet.
7. Creates an ideal environment for role-playing. A person can "be" someone or something other than what he is as he sings or moves (dances).
8. Can subtly induce the antisocial person to become increasingly involved with his peers. A socially retarded person, for example, can learn a skill that is accepted in public. Singing, dancing, or playing instruments can be a step toward group acceptance.
9. Affords a means through which aggressiveness can be lived out.
10. Creates a learning environment that can be noncompetitive. This implies few performance requirements of a strict or rigid nature.

Objectives of Music Therapy. The objectives of a music therpy program should reflect the function of music in combination with other avenues of experience, thus fostering total development of the person. The following statements of primary and secondary objectives illustrate the many possible aspects of a music program, and can serve as guides for establishing goals in many other situations. These objectives were developed for use at the Georgia Retardation Center in Atlanta.[1]

THERAPEUTIC MUSIC PROGRAM OBJECTIVES

A. As a result of the Music Program, students at the Georgia Retardation Center will attain the Primary Objectives of personal development that enables the individual to interact as a social being and will therefore:

1. Develop satisfactory social relationships through interaction with peers and adults in the numerous group experiences and environments provided for them.
2. Develop a likeable personality and a proper self-image in an atmosphere of contentment and acceptance offered in the musical setting, with opportunities for pleasurable, successful achievement building self-confidence and determination.
3. Develop an appreciation of the arts, with the desire and ability to express oneself creatively through various media.
4. Develop skill and the desire to be both spectator and participant in worthwhile leisure-time activities: sport, music, circus, parties, church, etc. both on campus and in the community.
5. Develop through music an awareness of the spirtual aspects of life.
6. Develop responsive vocalization and spontaneous expression through the musical stimuli which foster verbalization.

1. Taken from *The Role of the Clinical Music Program in an Inter-Disciplinary Setting,* Clinical Music Program, Donna Cypret, Director, Georgia Retardation Center, 1970. Used by permission.

7. Develop auditory discrimination and memory; learning many speech sounds; increasing vocabulary and rote learning.

8. Develop meaningful associations of spoken words with pictures, objects, people, action, direction, moving from the familiar to the new.

9. Develop concepts of shape, size, and relativity; large and small, identical or different, near and far, few and lot, long and short, etc., through the use of visual, auditory, and kinesthetic stimuli.

10. Develop control of movement and certain motor skills through the use of instruments and of movement to music.

11. Develop concept of relaxation and skilled coordination through musical activities (especially applicable to cerebral palsied students).

12. Develop happier, alert, and better motivated students even when musical growth is slight.

B. The Subsidiary Objectives of creating a capacity for musical activity:

1. Appreciation. Through numerous experiences in structured musical setting, it is hoped that every student at the Georgia Retardation Center will:
   (a) Respond in a sensitive way to the varied moods expressed by the music he hears, moves to, sings, and plays.
   (b) Participate in musical activities with enthusiasm, pleasure, and success.
   (c) Demonstrate potential for gaining meaning from the musical stimuli "Conceptualization."

2. *Musical competencies.* As a result of the Music Program, some students will:
   (a) *Listening*
      (1) Be aware of music, both live and recorded.
      (2) Respond to timbre of various instruments.
      (3) Recognize timbre of various instruments.
      (4) Respond to music that is of different styles, i.e., folk, serious, rock, country, sacred, etc.
      (5) Recognize music of different styles.
      (6) Respond to music of various media, i.e., orchestral, vocal, etc.
      (7) Recognize music of various media.
      (8) Respond to music of various tonalities, i.e., pentatonic scale, major scale, minor scale, whole-tone scale.
      (9) Recognize music of various tonalities.
      (10) Respond to basic contrasts in music, i.e., high and low, up and down, fast and slow, soft and loud, even and uneven, sound and silence, long and short.
      (11) Recognize basic contrasts in music.
   (b) *Singing*
      (1) Spontaneously vocalize tonal, rhythmic, or exclamatory sounds to composed songs.
      (2) Spontaneously vocalize improvised melodies expressing their own feelings.
      (3) Spontaneously verbalize improvised melodies expressing their own feelings.
      (4) Sing melodies or melodic fragments of composed songs in a recognizable manner.
      (5) Sing melodies or melodic fragments of composed songs on pitch.

(c) *Playing instruments*
  (1) Explore and experiment with various instruments.
  (2) Use instruments to follow the basic beat of melodies.
  (3) Use instruments (with or without assistance) to play the rhythm of the melody or melodic fragments.
  (4) Develop a beating pattern which is one of complete rhythmic freedom.
(d) *Moving to music*
  (1) Participate freely in action songs and singing games.
  (2) Dramatize song through characterization and bodily motion.
  (3) Respond to the rhythm of the music by performing with large bodily movement, i.e., walk, run, gallop, skip, jump.
  (4) Emphasize beat and rhythmic patterns by using a variety of physical responses, i.e., tap, clap, sway (with or without assistance).
(e) *Creativity*
  (1) Spontaneously improvise melodies by singing or playing instruments.
  (2) Spontaneously improvise rhythm patterns by singing or playing instruments.
  (3) Express the mood of music being sung or played through bodily movement.
  (4) Create additional words for songs he knows.
  (5) Participate in the creation and performance of musical playlets.

3. *Musical concepts.* As a result of the music program, some students will be able to develop a capacity for musical perception resulting in the formation of musical concepts and will therefore be able to:
(a) *Melody*
  (1) Distinguish melodic range as: high, medium, low.
  (2) Identify melodic direction in terms of: stepwise, skipwise, jump.
(b) *Rhythm*
  (1) Recognize contrasts in sound and silence.
  (2) Recognize contrasts in long and short.
  (3) Identify overall rhythmic movement as even or uneven.
  (4) Recognize short rhythmic phrases as same or different.
  (5) Recognize that music moves in groups of 2.
  (6) Recognize that music moves in groups of 3.
(c) *Harmony*
  (1) Recognize the presence of multiple sounds within a musical entity.
  (2) Reflect awareness of multiple sound by singing a melody with contrasting accompaniment.
  (3) Reflect awareness of multiple sounds by playing a melody with contrasting accompaniment.
  (4) Reflect awareness of multiple sounds by playing contrasting patterns as accompaniments to songs by ostinato.
  (5) Reflect awareness of multiple sounds by playing contrasting patterns as accompaniments to songs by cluster.
  (6) Reflect awareness of multiple sounds by playing contrasting patterns as accompaniments to songs by interval.
  (7) Reflect awareness of multiple sounds by playing contrasting patterns as accompaniments to songs by chord.

(d) *Form*

    (1) Identify melodic and rhythmic phrases as same or different.

    (2) Recognize sections within a composition as being same or different.

    (3) Reflect awareness of phrase in singing.

    (4) Demonstrate awareness of same-different phrases by selecting same-different instruments for accompaniment.

    (5) Indicate recognition of phrases by responding with appropriate body movements.

    (6) Develop contrasting movements appropriate for same-different sections or phrases.

    (7) Associate same-different geometric shapes with same-different phrases or sections.

(e) *Expressions*

    (1) Recognize contrasts in dynamics—loud and soft.

    (2) Recognize contrasts in tempo—fast-slow.

    (3) Identify some common orchestral instruments.

    (4) Associate instruments with appropriate high-low category.

    (5) Learn to associate musical sounds with particular moods when selecting instruments for accompaniments.

    (6) Indicate awareness of overall mood in dance movements.

    (7) Choose appropriate instruments when adding sound effects to stories and poetry or when creating accompaniments for familiar songs.

Music Therapy involves many integrative processes. These comprise elements which may be physical, psychological, or physiological. For this reason, persons specializing in Music Therapy as a career should have in-depth training. This is especially important in the areas of psychological functioning.

Many recreational leaders are trained in physical education programs which emphasize motor and physical skills. Such persons are frequently involved in recreation programs which have an adjunct of rehabilitation in terms of muscular and functional development. From that standpoint, it seems appropriate to include in this book a discussion of therapeutic music as related to the treatment of such problems as mobility, endurance, and coordination. These aspects make up the general area known as functional therapy.

There are multiple uses for music as functional therapy. They are most often reflected in rehabilitation work with muscular-coordinative skills. Among these are to (1) increase mobility, (2) lengthen endurance, and (3) develop coordination.

The term *coordination* covers a wide area. It includes eye-hand coordination, hand-foot coordination, hand-arm coordination, and so forth. Musical activities can assist in all of these problems. Reciprocal patterns, such as those involved in walking, may also be treated in a functional program.

The purpose is to link music with physical-functional conditions as a corrective device. Specific musical instruments can be used to increase mobility or to establish conditions for greater endurance. In fact, with occupational therapy as a foundation. The use of musical instruments is sometimes the essential part of functional therapy. A detailed summary of musical activities directly related to the clinical treatment of mobility, endurance, and coordinative problems may be found in Appendix E, pp. 177-184.

MUSIC THERAPY FOR THE RETARDED

There is increasing national attention given to retardation. Many agencies, including the schools, are devoting considerable effort in meeting the needs of retarded persons. The goals and objectives of music within retardation programs have been advanced by substantial numbers of music therapists. They are found to be of considerable importance in carrying out a successful program. An excellent example of the comprehensiveness of such a set of objectives is easily seen in the quoted portion from the Georgia Retardation Center given on pp. 32-35.

Another excellent statement of objectives and suggested teaching approaches is that prepared by Marjorie Reeves for the schools of Illinois. As quoted from this publication the primary objective of music is "to provide every child the opportunity to experience music and express himself through music to the best of his ability . . . , the key is 'to the best of his ability.' "[2]

Most music programs for retarded persons reflect the philosophy that therapeutic music involves a learning process coincidental with the needs of retardation. These include a wide range of experiences which imply learning by doing.

A low I.Q. does not eliminate a person's need to be creative. In fact, the retarded should be encouraged to discover their own level of expressive creativity. The music therapist must always remember that the quality of the product created is unimportant. The main concern here is spontaneity and freedom. These factors allow expression through various musical activities. Some implications derived from the functional use of music for the retarded follow.

1. Improving recognition of abstract symbols through association of signs with auditory stimuli.
2. Lengthening of ability span through gradually prolonging participation in listening and playing.
3. Developing a wider range of ideas through imagery and dramatization.
4. Enlarging the scope of social interaction by physical response in a group as in folk dancing.
5. Opportunities to "belong" with others in group performing situations.
6. Realization of the similarity among all persons of demands for regulation of behavier in accepted ways since musical experiences can require adherence to a notated score, or to a set of musical principles and aural values.

SUGGESTED ACTIVITIES

Aside from the use of music to foster learning skills, achieving purely musical goals and clinical uses, music possesses unique recreational qualities. These are largely the concern of the recreation director in clinical settings.

Two principles of Music Therapy emphasized by E. Thayer Gaston, recognized authority in the field of Music Therapy are:
1. The establishment of interpersonal relationships (social skills).
2. The bringing about of self-esteem (positive self-image).

Through purely recreational activities, music can assist in actualizing these worthwhile principles. To foster social relationships among special learners the following are suggestions from which a recreation director might select activities to fit the needs of his group.

---

2. Marjorie Reeves, *Music for Handicapped Children* (Springfield Illinois: Office of Public Instruction, n.d.). Distributed by Instructional Materials Center for Handicapped Children and Youth, 1020 South Spring Street, Springfield, Illinois 63704.

1. Playing name games. Singing a person's name on pitches as the class gestures in that person's direction and matching the pitches used when singing back the person's name.

2. Organize singing games so children can indicate their choice of partners by gesture. This helps create an atmosphere of social interaction.

3. Employ ball-bouncing to music in which the players are invited to pass or bounce the ball to another.

4. Children form a circle with one child in the center. To the beat of a drum, the children follow whatever movement the one in the center is performing. As the game progresses, the one in the center selects a child in the circle to replace him or her.

5. Children sit on the floor in a circle and, to the beat of a drum, pass a bean bag first to the right until the bag has made a complete circle, then to the left. Eventually, replace the drum beat with a recording of a strong Strauss waltz or Sousa march.

6. Use songs in which a child's name can be substituted to personalize the experience. Examples are: "Oh, where have you been Billy Boy?" can be sung using the name of one of the boys in the class or "Swing your partner, skip to my Lou" can be sung using the name of one of the girls. With a little imagination and selecting certain songs this technique can accomplish much to bring about a feeling of social awareness.

7. Select songs that can be mimed or dramatized by various members of the class to instigate interaction among the group. Examples of this kind of song are: "O, Soldier, Soldier Won't You Marry Me?" "The Twelve Days of Christmas," and "In a Cabin In the Wood."

8. Employ the technique called "Mirroring" which involves two children standing face to face with only eye contact. As they listen to selected music, invite them to move in place without touching. One child "mirrors" the movements of the other in this manner. Then they change so the other does the mirroring. It is strongly suggested to use quiet, easy flowing music such as Satie's "Gymnopedie #3" and Debussy's "Clair de Lune." Do not use music that is sung, as words have a strong tendency to interfere with allowing only the music to dictate movement.

9. Invite children to participate in group musical activities such as large group singing and dancing.

10. Instigate concert attendance with a group of children. If possible, after the experience, ask the children to share their feelings about the performance with each other.

11. Using a very large square silk scarf, have one child hold each corner. By experimenting with various ways they might manipulate the scarf through interaction to create interesting effects, they then begin to feel the need and desire to cooperate with each other to achieve these effects. While the children are involved in this activity, be certain to use instrumental music of a rather calm nature. As control and awareness are reached, other types of music can be used with various tempo changes.

12. Music, being a form of nonverbal communication, can lead children to carry on a "conversation" with each other using drums instead of words. This question and answer technique tends to draw them closer to each other. As they become familiar with the activity, have them converse with each other on pitch instruments such as bells, metallophones, and xylophones. Finally, transfer this technique into movement. One child can move his or her question and the partner will respond with some form of individual movement.

To nurture a feeling of self esteem in a recreational setting for the special learner, the person in charge must create a very positive, informal and non-threatening atmosphere. All that is planned must insure success so that those children involved can receive an instant feeling of acceptable accomplishment and importance. The following are some suggestions of ways this might be established.

1. When a child "creates" an interesting movement responding to whatever is being done, call attention to it and give that child much praise and reenforcement in front of the class.
2. Have the class sing a song that requires only one chord on the autoharp and ask a child to accompany while the class sings. This child should be made to feel very important.
3. Giving various children opportunities to play on percussion instruments at appropriate places in songs that are being sung by the class.
4. When pentatonic literature is used, invite a child to accompany the class by playing a bourdon (interval of an open fifth) on a metallophone or xylophone.
5. Encourage all children to explore various classroom instruments during their leisure time and share their discoveries with the class.
6. Invite a child to act as the conductor and lead the class in a familiar song. Be sure to tell the class to watch the conductor very carefully. Give that child much praise when the song is finished.

SUMMARY

One cannot say that music is therapeutic in itself. It is useful because of the psychological and physiological effects it has on mood and behavior. Used therapeutically, therefore, music is not an end in itself, but rather a means to treatment. It also enables the person to make better use of other experiences.

Music Therapy involves two areas. The first is music itself; this includes music lessons, practice of technique, and the use of certain pieces to produce various responses. The second is the relationship developed between the instructor and patient. Using the flexible medium of his special field, the instructor is an effective therapeutic agent. The atmosphere which he creates, and the relationship he establishes, make music an activity in the therapeutic sense.

Used therapeutically, musical experiences can often cause patients to acquire new and lasting interests in the art itself. In other words, it can be enjoyed as a pastime bringing satisfaction and enrichment long after its educational and therapeutic uses are over.

SUGGESTED ASSIGNMENTS AND PROJECTS

1. Make a list of song that might be beneficial in a psychological way for use in clinical settings.
2. Check with the authorities in your public school system to discover ways music is used to assist learning in Special Education classes.
3. What ways can you visualize performance situations in music that would have positive connotations in the process of mainstreaming.
4. List five ways music can be used to increase a person's self image.

SELECTED REFERENCES

ANTEY, JOHN W. *Sing and Learn.* New York: The John Day Co. 1965.
BITCON, CAROL H. *Alike and Different.* Santa Anna, California: Rosha Press, 1976.
CANNER, NORMAN and HARRIET KLEBANOFF. *And a Time to Dance.* Boston: Beacon Press, 1968.
CARLSON, BERNIECE, and DAVID GINGLAND. *Recreation for Retarded Teenagers and Young Adults.* Nashville, Tenn.: Abingdon Press, 1968.

COLE, FRANCES. *Music for Children with Special Needs*. Glendale, California: Bowmar Publishing Co., 1965.

The Expressive Arts for Mentally Retarded. National Association for Retarded Children, Inc., New York, 1967.

GASTON, E. THAYER. *Music in Therapy*. New York, New York: The Macmillan Co., 1968.

GINGLAND, DAVID, and WINIFRED STILES. *Music Activities for Retarded Children*. Nashville, Tenn.: Abingdon Press, 1965.

GOTTLIEB, J. *Educating Mentally Retarded Persons in the Mainstream*. Baltimore, Md.: University Park Press, 1980.

HARBERT, WILHELMINA K. *Opening Doors Through Music*. Springfield, Illinois: Charles C Thomas Publisher, 1974.

HUNT, VALERIE V. *Recreation for the Handicapped*. Englewood Cliffs, New Jersey: Prentice-Hall Inc., 1955.

KOLSTOE, OLIVER. *Teaching Educable Mentally Retarded Children*. Holt Publishing Co., 1970.

MICHEL, DONALD E. *Music Therapy*. Springfield, Illinois: Charles C Thomas Publisher, 1977.

MORAN, MARY ROSS. *Assessment of the Exceptional Learner in the Regular Classroom*. Denver, Colorado: Love Publishing Co., 1978.

"Music As Therapy." (issure) *Musical Journal*, November, 1970.

Music for the Exceptional Child. Compiled by Richard M. Graham. Reston, Virginia: Music Educators National Conference, 1975.

Music in Developmental Therapy. Edited by Jennie Purvis and Shelley Samet. Baltimore, Maryland: University Park Press, 1976.

NOCERA, SONA D. *Reaching the Special Learner Through Music*. Morristown, New Jersey: Silver Burdett Co., 1979.

NORDOFF, PAUL, and ROBBINS C. *Music Therapy for Handicapped Children*. New York: Rudolf Steiner Pub., 1965.

ROBINS, FERRIS, and JENNET ROBINS. *Education Rhythmics for Mentally and Physically Handicapped Children*. New York: Association Press. 1967.

SCHATTNER, REGINA. *Creative Dramatics for Handicapped*. New York: The John Day Co., 1967.

WEDEMEYER, AVARIL, and JOYCE CEJKA. *Creative Ideas for Teaching Exceptional Children*. Denver, Colorado: Love Publishing Co., 1975.

ZIMMER, LOWELL JAY. *Music Handbook for the Child in Special Education*. Hackensack, New Jersey: Joseph Boonin, Inc., 1976.

RECORDINGS

Activity and Game Songs, Vols. I, II and III by Tom Glazer. CMS Records, Inc., New York, New York 10007.

The Feel of Music by Hap Palmer. Educational Activities, Inc., Freeport, New York 11520.

Getting to Know Myself, by Hap Palmer. Educational Activities, Inc., Freeport, Long Island, New York, New York 11520.

Happy Time Listening, by William T. Braley. Educational Activities, Inc., Freeport, Long Island, New York, New York 11520.

Ideas, Thoughts and Feelings, by Hap Palmer. Educational Activities, Inc., Freeport, Long Island, New York, New York 11520.

I Know the Colors in the Rainbow, by Ella Jenkins. Educational Activities, Inc., Freeport, Long Island, New York, New York 11520.

It's About Time, by Avon Gillespie. Educational Activities, Inc., Freeport, Long Island, New York, New York 11520.

Let's Sing Fingerplays by Tom Glazer. CMS Records, Inc. New York, New York 10007.

Looking Back and Looking Forward by Ella Jenkins. Educational Activities, Inc., Freeport, Long Island, New York, New York 11520.

Movin' by Hap Palmer. Educational Activities, Inc., Freeport, Long Island, New York, New York 11520.

Music for Every Child: Vol. I All Aboard!, Vol. 2 Together We Go! Vol. 3 Room for Everybody! by Dr. Ruth De Cesare. Educational Activities, Inc., Freeport, Long Island, New York, New York 11520.

Music for 1's & 2's by Tom Glazer. CMS Records, Inc., New York, New York 10007.

Music Skills by Pam Tims and Gary Gassell. Melody House, Oklahoma City, Oklahoma 73114.

Oooo We're Having Fun by David White. Tom Thumb Records, Rhythms Productions, Los Angeles, California 90034.

Pretend by Hap Palmer. Educational Activities, Inc., Freeport, Long Island, New York, New York 11520.

Quiet Time by Harrell C. Lucky. Melody House, Oklahoma City, Oklahoma 73114.

Raindrops by Sharon Lucky. Melody House, Oklahoma City, Oklahoma 73114.

The Rhythm Makers by Ruth and David White. Rhythms Productions, Los Angeles, California 90034.

Songs for Children with Special Needs. Bowmar Records, Inc., Glendale, California 91201.

Time After Time by Avon Gillispie. Educational Activities, Inc., Freeport, New York 11520.

You'll Sing a Song and I'll Sing a Song by Ella Jenkins. Folkways Records Englewood Cliffs, New Jersey 17632.

II.

instructional ideas
and programs

The types of musical activities in recreational programs reflect considerable variety in instructional needs, procedures, levels of accomplishment, and material resources. For each specialized area, there are published sources to provide teaching ideas and experiences. This part of the text includes illustrated descriptions of activities which often form the basic for music programs in such areas as parks, camps, and community centers. They are organized under the following headings: (1) group singing and song leadership, (2) instrumental accompaniment, (3) sound exploration and choral speaking, and (4) dramatic movement and traditional dancing, (5) Playing a Small Wind Instrument, (6) Finding, Making and Using Your Own Instrument, (7) Music and Olympics.

9.

group singing and song leadership

Probably the most rewarding musical experience within a recreational setting is group singing. It provides a music-making experience for persons of all ages and abilities. And, because there is no audience as such, individuals usually become involved without embarrassment or self-consciousness.

The most important single person in any group singing activity is the song leader. His functions are directly related to the needs, interests, and musical capabilities of the group. These may range from indoor auditorium song fests to outdoor camp sings.

The musical abilities within groups will reflect considerable diversity. In some groups, many persons may be able to harmonize by ear or read music with fluency. In others, even a single melody line may be difficult to learn well. For this reason, the song leader must be flexible enough to handle the limitations and aspirations in each group as he finds them.

LEARNING NEW SONGS

Besides learning songs with a book or other visual aid, there will be times when leaders will want to teach new songs by imitation (rote). In fact, recreational singing often requires rote approaches.

The particular style and form of the song determines the nature of the teaching approach. Also, it is good to use a variety of plans to maintain interest. Any one or combination of the following suggestions may be useful depending on the type of song being presented.

1. Leader sings the entire song. Some textural or musical aspect is discussed or pointed out.
2. Leader sings the song phrase by phrase and the group repeats without breaking the rhythm.
3. Group responds on a repeated section that is simple and easily remembered.
4. Group taps or claps the rhythm of the words as the leader repeats the song.
5. Group hums along on the tune before learning words or new verses.
6. Group responds to all or parts of the song with instruments.
7. Group follows musical phrases to recall which are alike and which are different.
8. Group learns by imitation from a recording.

When using any of the approaches above, there are always additional considerations which contribute to the enjoyment and success of the community singing.

1. The song leader should be very familiar with all of the songs to be presented. These should reflect variety and follow thoughtful organization in terms of the singing order. The interests and enjoyment of the group are the primary considerations.

2. A successful leader should project enthusiasm by his physical countenance and the clarity of his conducting. He should be able to use the conventional techniques and know when each is appropriate.

3. The starting pitch of each song should be well established for the group. A chord giving the tonality (key of the song) can be played on a piano, or other accompanying instrument. The starting tone or pitch of the first word can also be given.

4. When presenting new songs, groups sometimes need a visual aid to assist with the song texts such as inexpensive song sheets, 35 mm slides, or overhead transparencies. The versatility of each depends on the size of the group and the physical arrangement of the room.

5. A good accompaniment for group singing is a must. Generally a competent pianist should be on hand to maintain the rhythmic flow, the tonality, and the expressiveness of the song. The accompanist often plays a brief introduction which sets the mood and song style.

6. Pace each song session to keep and hold a high interest level in the group. Try not to dwell too long on any single song—especially if it is new. Long or difficult new songs need not be perfected in one session. Present them a little at a time by adding clapping to the rhythm, whistling a portion, or humming along on a verse until it becomes familiar. Eventually, it will be one of the group's "old favorites."

7. When introducing a new round, teach it first as a unison song. Be cautious about dividing it into a round too soon, or using too many sections for round singing. Two or three sections are sufficient. Each section should sing the round as many times as there are sections into which the group has been divided.

8. Many singing groups enjoy song sessions which are built around a theme or topic, such as "Christmas in Many Lands"; "Songs of National Origin"; "A Trip Around the World"; "Tin Pan Alley"; "Names in Songs" ("Bill Baily," "Lili Marlene," "Alfie" etc.).

9. It often adds to a song session if the leader can intersperse anecdotes about the songs. Good leaders usually collect interesting bits of information for this purpose. But regardless of how interesting these are, the use of verbal remarks should be kept at a minimum.

10. Interest is high when talented members of the group perform special solos or ensembles. It adds variety to group singing and provides an opportunity to "launch" the male quartet or ladies' sextet.

CONDUCTING PATTERNS

The ability to conduct basic patterns is an important requisite for all song leaders. There are, however, occasions when formal conducting can be set aside in favor of more informal ways of keeping time. Some of these might include simple time beating, foot tapping, finger snapping, body gesture, accompaniment, or lead-in cues, such as "one, two, ready—sing."

Formal conducting patterns relate directly to the meter signature of a song. Below are examples of meter signatures and the manual pattern used in conducting each.[1] A song to practice each conducting pattern is also included.

Meter Signature

$$\frac{2}{4} \quad \text{or fast} \quad \frac{6}{8} \quad \text{(duple in 2's)}$$

Conducting Pattern

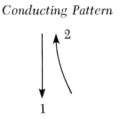

Under the Spreading Chestnut Tree

ENGLAND

Un - der the spread - ing chest - nut tree,

When I held you on my knee,

We were hap - py as can be,

Un - der the spread - ing chest - nut tree.

Additional songs in duple meter which may be conducted with the above pattern:

Skip to My Lou
Are You Sleeping
Shoo Fly
Yankee Doodle
Kookaburra
This Old Man
Dixie
Sailing, Sailing
When Johnny Comes Marching Home
Silent Night

Old Mac Donald Had a Farm
Jingle Bells
She'll Be Comin' Round the Mountain
Lightly Row
The Marines' Hymn
Oh Susannah
Row, Row, Row Your Boat
Pussy Cat
Over the River and Through the Wood

1. Music and texts of all songs listed are in Dallin-Dallin *Heritage Songster*, 2nd ed., published by Wm. C. Brown Company Publishers, Dubuque, Iowa, 1980.

Meter Signature   *Conducting Pattern*

3   3
4   2   (triple in 3's)

Music Alone Shall Live

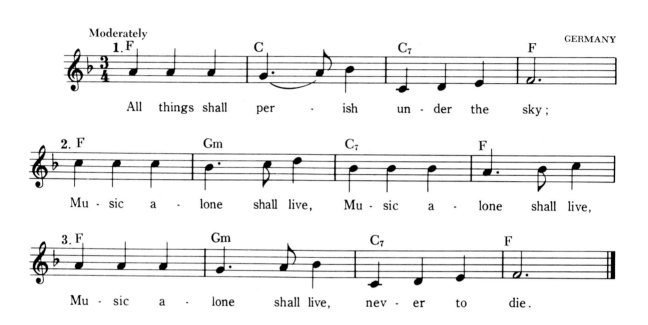

Himmel und Erde müssen vergehn;
Aber die Musica, aber die Musica,
Aber die Musica, bleiben bestehn.

Additional songs in triple meter which may be conducted with the above pattern:

America
Oh, Where, Oh, Where Has My Little Dog
    Gone?
Prayer of Thanksgiving
Lavender's Blue Dilly, Dilly
Happy Birthday to You
Come Thou Almighty King
Oh, How Lovely Is the Evening
Sidewalks of New York
On Top of Old Smoky

The Star Spangled Banner
Skaters' Waltz (Waldteufel)
Sweet Betsy from Pike
We Wish You a Merry Christmas
The First Noel
Down in the Valley
Clementine
Faith of Our Fathers
Daisy Bell

Meter Signature   *Conducting Pattern*

4
4   (Quadruple in 4's)

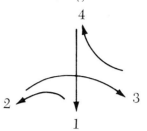

Aura Lee

U. S.

1. As the black-bird in the spring, 'Neath the wil-low tree,_____

Sat and piped, I heard him sing, Sing - ing Au - ra Lee.

Chorus

Au - ra Lee, Au - ra Lee, Maid of gold - en hair,

Sun-shine came a - long with thee, And swal-lows in the air.

2. In her blush the rose was born,
Music when she spoke,
In her eyes the glow of morn
Into splendor broke.

Additional songs in quadruple meter conducted with the above pattern:

America, the Beautiful   I've Been Work on the Railroad
All Through the Night   Twinkle, Twinkle Little Star
Long, Long Ago   Hark the Herald Angels Sing
A-Hunting We Will Go   Red River Valley
O Come All Ye Faithful   Crusaders' Hymn
Alouette   Swing Low, Sweet Chariot
Jacob's Ladder   London Bridge
Auld Lang Syne

There are some songs written in $\frac{6}{8}$ meter which are intended to be sung at a moderate to slow tempo. These songs require the conducting pattern shown below if and when they are sung slowly.

Meter Signature   *Conducting Pattern*

$\frac{6}{8}$ (Sextuple in 6's)

Greensleeves

Greensleeves

Christ   the   Lord,__ the   Son ___ the   Babe ___ of   Ma - ry.

Additional songs in sextuple meter which may be conducted with the above pattern:

We Three Kings   Silent Night
Sweet and Low   Greensleeves

One of the important responsibilies of a song leader is to bring all of the singers together for a clean, confident start on the first word of a song. This is comparatively easy when songs begin on a down-beat (usually the first beat of the measure). The leader may conduct one full measure to establish the tempo and direct the singers to begin on the first beat of his second conducted measure. Sometimes he can say, "One, two, ready, sing" in strict cadence as a verbal starting cue. Or he may give a clear preparatory beat in strict rhythm on the last beat of the measure preceding entrance.

However, when a song begins on the up-beat (usually the last beat in a measure), entrances are frequently weak and ragged. One way to overcome this is for the leader to conduct all beats occurring prior to the entrance up-beat. Until the group becomes used to this technique, the leader can count as he conducts. The following common examples can be used for practice. These are upbeats on the third and fourth beats of the measure.

Songs starting on an up-beat in a 3 or triple rhythm:

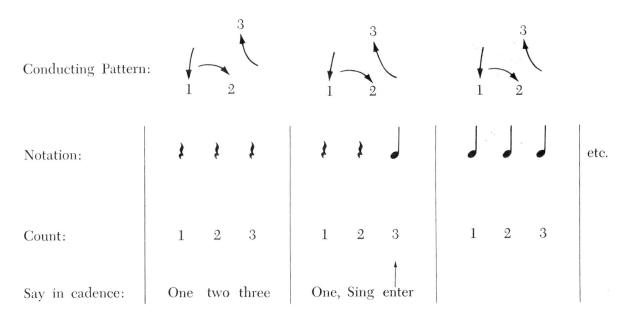

The Holly and the Ivy

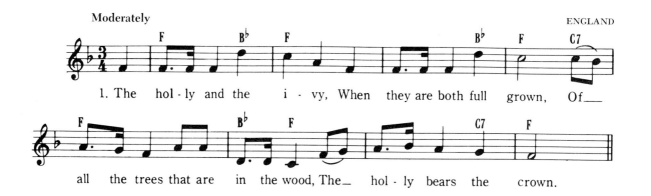

Songs starting on an up-beat in a 4 or quadruple rhythm:

Conducting Pattern:

Notation:

Count:

Say in Cadence:

| One two three four | One two sing enter |

Auld Lang Syne

Auld Lang Syne

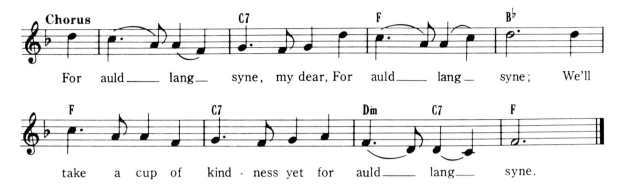

Additional songs starting on the last (up) beat of the measure:

America, The Beautiful
On Top of Old Smoky
The Star Spangled Banner
Oh Where, Oh Where Has My Little Dog
    Gone?
Prayer of Thanksgiving
The First Noel
Happy Birthday to You
The Marines' Hymn
Clementine

Bingo
The More We Get Together
Flow Gently Sweet Afton
Sweet Betsy from Pike
We Wish You a Merry Christmas
Greensleeves
Oh, A-Hunting We Will Go
Oh Come All Ye Faithful
Oh Susannah
Red River Valley

ADDING SIMPLE HARMONY PARTS TO SONGS

Harmonic enrichment can turn an otherwise routine song session into a rewarding and sensitive experience. Community singing in any recreational situation seems to take on a special quality when groups sing in harmony. There are numerous ways to add simple patterns to familiar songs thereby producing harmonic effects. Perhaps the easiest harmonic experience is antiphonal singing. The following songs are examples of answer-back or "antiphonal" singing.

Old Texas

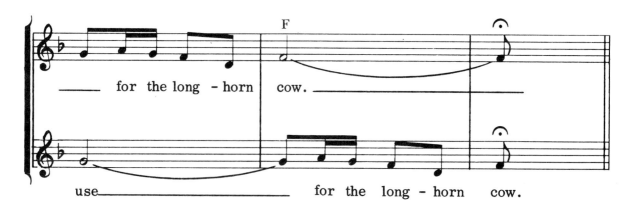

They've plowed and fenced my cattle range,
And the people there are all so strange.
I'll take my horse, I'll take my rope,
And hit the trail upon a lope.
Say adios to the Alamo,
And turn my head toward Mexico.

For further enrichment, simple repeated patterns (*ostinati*), such as shown below, can be sung or played throughout.

Sing:
Play:
(Woodblock,
bells or bongo)

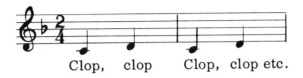

Clop, clop   Clop, clop etc.

Let's Sing a Song

AMERICAN FOLK
WORDS JMB

Besides answer-back songs, repeated vocal patterns can go along with certain songs. The following *ostinati* patterns may be added to "Home on the Range." Indicate the pattern that fits with the words of the melody by using either a visual cue or hand signal. The number of the pattern is indicated above the appropriate sections of the text.

Rid-ing a - long

(1)   (2)
Oh give me a home where the buffalo roam,
(1)   (1)
Where the deer and the antelope play;
(1)   (2)
Where seldom is heard a discouraging word,
(1)   (3)
And the skies are not cloudy all day.

Rid-ing a - long

(1)   (1)
Home, home on the range
(1)   (1)
Where the dear and the antelope play;
(1)   (2)
Where seldom is heard a discouraging word,
(1)   (3)
And the skies are not cloudy all day.

Rid-ing a - long

PARTNER SONGS

Partner songs can provide a further enrichment to a song session. These are songs that can be sung together because they have the same harmonic structure. A singing group can be divided into two, three or four parts with each part singing a different song at the same time. Songs that harmonize in this manner may be selected from the following list:

Three Blind Mice
John Brown Had a Little Indian
Row, Row, Row Your Boat
Skip To My Lou
Are You Sleeping?
Hail, Hail the Gang's All Here
The Farmer in the Dell
Bow, Bow, Bow Belinda

The following two songs illustrate the above technique. Add to the enjoyment of group singing by putting the appropriate gestures with the words as indicated.

First, have everyone learn the songs thoroughly. Then, practice the gestures. When everyone feels confident, have one group sing, "Harry Armstrong" while the other group sings, "Tony Chestnut" employing all the gestures. Finally, ask both groups to "think" or sense (internalize) the song without actually singing it but go through the motions in correct rhythm. This is an interesting activity with camping groups, senior citizens and, especially, with Special Education situations.

Harry Armstrong

WORDS AND MUSIC
J. M. BATCHELLER

Har-ry Arm-strong took a jour-ney, Har-ry's back, Har-ry's back. Har-ry

Arm-strong took a jour-ney Now, our Har-ry's back.

Tony Chestnut

WORDS COURTESY
OF GRACE NASH

To-ny Chest-nut knows I love him, To-ny knows, To-ny knows.

To-ny Chest-nut knows I love him, That's what To-ny knows.

HARRY ARMSTRONG

HARRY ARM----STRONG
(point to hair) (point to arm) (flex bicep ala Popeye)

TOOK A JOURNEY
(both hands steer an auto wheel) (point to knee)

HARRY'S BACK
(point to hair) (point to back)

(Repeat same motions for remainder of song)

TONY CHESTNUT

TO----NY CHEST---NUT
(point to toes) (knee) (cross hands on chest) (head)

KNOWS I LOVE HIM
(point to nose) (point to eye) (hug self)

(Repeat same motions for remainder of song)

Easy tenor and bass parts can also be added. The following is a good example which is suitable for all age groups. Harmony parts may be added one at a time in a rhythmic fashion. Chording instruments are also very appropriate.[2]

Rock-a-my-Soul

2. Arrangements as found in Sally Monsour and Margaret Perry, *A Junior High School Music Handbook*, 2nd ed. (Englewood Cliffs, New Jersey: Prentice-Hall, Inc., 1970), pp. 81-82.

Rock-a-my-Soul

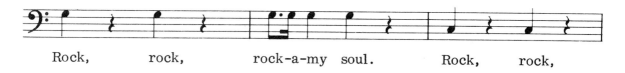

Rock,   rock,   rock-a-my soul.   Rock,   rock,

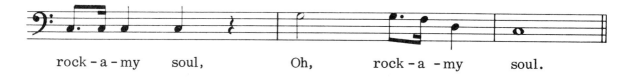

rock - a - my   soul,   Oh,   rock - a - my   soul.

A parody on a familiar song can add fun and satisfaction to recreational singing. These are especially useful during holiday seasons. If the singing group is made up of youngsters, they will be anxious to make up their own sets of words. The following may serve as examples.

Tune: "Are You Sleeping?"[3]
(Thanksgiving)

Turkey 'n' dressing, Turkey 'n' dressing
Pumpkin pie, Pumpkin pie.
Everybody's humming, Thanksgiving is coming
Yum, yum, yum; yum, yum, yum.

Tune: "Did You Ever See a Lassie?"
(Halloween)

Oh, once I had a pumpkin, a pumpkin, a pumpkin
Oh, once I had a pumpkin, with no face at all.
With no eyes, and no nose and no mouth and no teeth,
Oh, once I had a pumpkin with no face at all.
So I made a Jack-o-lantern, Jack-o-lantern, Jack-o-lantern
So I made a Jack-o-lantern with a big funny face.
With big eyes, and big nose and big mouth and big teeth.
So I made a Jack-o-lantern with a big funny face.

Tune: "Farmer in the Dell"
(Halloween)

The witch rides tonight, the witch rides tonight.
Hi Ho it's Halloween, the witch rides tonight.
The witch takes a bat, the witch takes a bat,
Hi Ho it's Halloween, the witch takes a bat.
The bat takes a cat, the bat takes a cat,
Hi Ho it's Halloween, the bat takes a cat.
The cat scares the ghost, the cat scares the ghost,
Hi Ho it's Halloween, the cat scares the ghost.
The ghosts dance around, the ghosts dance around
Hi Ho it's Halloween, the ghosts dance around, Boo!

3. Sybal Parr, Atlanta Georgia. Used by permission.

The literature for group singing includes every type of song. To assist the recreational song leader, lists of songs by category may be found in Appendix H. The songs which follow are good examples for group singing. Practice them for using various techniques for rote learning and for song conducting and leadership.

Sing Together

Vive L'amour

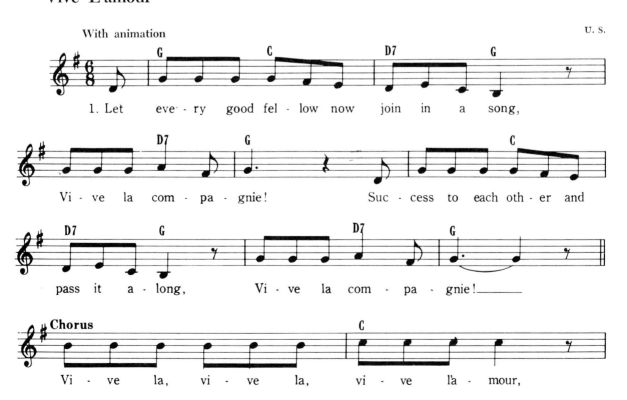

Vive L'amour

2. A friend on the left and a friend on the right, Vive la compagnie!
   In willing endeavor our hands we unite, Vive la compagnie!
3. Should time or occasion compel us to part, Vive la compagnie!
   These days shall forever enliven the heart, Vive la compagnie!

We're All Together Again

SELECTED REFERENCES

1. BECKMAN, FREDERICK. *Partner Songs and More Partner Songs.* Boston: Ginn and Co., 1962.
2. DALLIN, LEON and LYNN DALLIN. *Folk Songster* and *Heritage Songster.* Dubuque, Iowa: Wm. C. Brown Publisher, 1972.
3. LANDECK, BEATRICE and ELIZABETH CROOK. *Wake Up and Sing!* New York: Edward B. Marks Music Corp., 1969.
4. NYE, ROBERT et al. *Singing With Children.* Belmont, California: Wadsworth Publishing Co., 1970.
5. NYE, VERNICE T., et al. *Toward World Understanding With Song.* Belmont, California: Wadsworth Publishing Co., 1967.
6. *World Around Song Collections.* Burnsville, N. C. (Many collections of songs from around the world.)

Note: The following music series publications provide a multitude of songs appropriate for various groups and occasions.

BOARDMAN, EUNICE, and BARBARA ANDRESS. *Exploring Music,* K-8. New York: Holt, Rinhart and Winston, 1975. Also Boardman, Eunice and Barabra Andress. *The Music Book,* K-8. New York: Holt, Rinehart, and Winston, 1981.

BURTON, LEON, et al. *Comprehensive Musicianship through Classroom Music,* K-7. Menlo Park, Calif.: Addison-Wesley, 1975.

CHOATE, ROBERT, et al. *New Dimensions in Music,* K-8. New York: American Book Co., 1976.

EISMAN, LAWRENCE, et al. *Making Music Your Own,* 7 and 8. Morristown, N. J.: Silver Burdett Co., 1971.

LANDECK, BEATRICE, ELIZABETH CROOK, and HAROLD C. YOUNGBERG. *Making Music Your Own,* K-6. Morristown, N. J.: Silver Burdett Co., 1971.

LEONHARD, CHARLES, et al. *Discovering Music Together,* K-8. Chicago: Follett Publishing Co., 1970.

MARSH, MARY VAL, et al. *The Spectrum of Music,* K-8. New York: Macmillan Co., 1974.

REIMER, BENNETT, et al. *Silver Burdett Music,* K-8. Morristown, N. J.: Silver Burdett Co., 1974.

SUR, WILLIAM R., et al. *This is Music for Today,* K-8. Rockleigh, N. J.: Allyn and Bacon, 1970.

WERSEN, LOUIS, et al. *The Magic of Music,* K-6. Boston: Ginn and Co., 1963.

WILSON, HARRY, et al. *Growing with Music,* K-8. Related arts edition. Englewood Cliffs, N. J.: Prentice-Hall, 1970.

10.

instrumental accompaniment

The instruments which accompany group music-making provide an important means for attaining musical achievement and involvement.[1] For example, groups accompanying singing on the autoharp, uke, guitar, piano, or recorder, are sought after sources of enjoyment for many people. In fact, most recreation programs offer group instrument instruction for beginners of different ages.[2]

THE AUTOHARP

Probably the simplest accompanying instrument to play is the autoharp. It is easily mastered and can be self-taught. Because of its size and weight, it is an ideal instrument for recreational use. Its portability provides a means of accompaniment on hikes, around the campfire, in the recreational hall, at the beach, or at the dinner table. Besides being portable, it is relatively inexpensive when compared to a piano, violin, or accordion. The upkeep is no problem, and the tuning of the instrument is simple.

The autoharp is equipped with all the accessories for playing and tuning. Several picks are included to produce various degrees and kinds of sound effects. A shoulder strap is also supplied for playing while walking or standing.

Playing the Autoharp. The autoharp is usually played on the lap or on a table in front of the player. The wide part of the instrument is at the player's right. The left hand is used

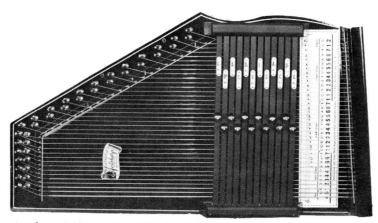

Autoharp is the registered Trade Mark of Oscar Schmidt International, Inc., Jersey City, New Jersey.

1. Special mention should be made of a comprehensive book on using instruments of all types in musical situations: Marguerite V. Hood, *Teaching Rhythm and Using Classroom Instruments* (Englewood Cliffs, New Jersey: Prentice-Hall, Inc., 1970).
2. For a listing of sources on playing instruments, see Appendix D, p. 117.

to depress the bars before the chord is strummed. The bars are clearly labeled identifying the various chords the instrument is capable of producing. (A twelve bar instrument is usually sufficient for recreational purposes.) The player's right hand strums away from the body, across the wire strings on either side of the bar rack. The sound created by strumming on the left side of the bar rack has a deep, full quality. The number of times the player strums depends on the beat pattern of the song and the player's own sense of rhythm, but the chord button must be changed when the harmony changes are indicated in the music.

Tuning the Autoharp. A tuning wrench is provided with each instrument. This wrench can easily be applied to the clearly marked pegs in order to tighten or loosen the attached string until the sound (pitch) corresponds to the pitch on a piano or tuning pipe.

Finding Chords on An Autoharp. On the twelve-bar autoharp the player can create accompaniments for three major keys (C, G, and F) and two minor keys (D, and A). Each of these keys has three bars which, when depressed, will create a tonic, subdominant and dominant-seventh chord (I, IV, V₇). The player must firmly press the bar representing the chord and then, with his right hand, strum the wire strings away from the body. Most editions of recreation songs have the chord symbols printed over the word or beat of the measure where a chord change is required.

When using the autoharp as the accompaniment for group singing, it is desirable to play a chordal introduction for each song. This can be done by strumming the three basic chords for the key in which the song is written, then plucking the single string for the opening pitch of the song. This helps the group keep in tune from the start as they sing each song.

There are many other interesting uses for the autoharp. One, by plucking or scraping the strings in various ways, interesting effects can be achieved, to be added to creating sound images and backgrounds for sound exploration and choral speaking situations. Also, by "drumming" on the strings with a wooden mallet or several wooden mallets grouped together, an effective percussive quality can be obtained for use with certain rousing and martial songs. The chords would be changed throughout the song in the same manner as for conventional strumming.

The following songs are illustrations. Sing along and strum as each chord change is indicated. The slanted lines indicate the strumming rhythm.

One Chord Song

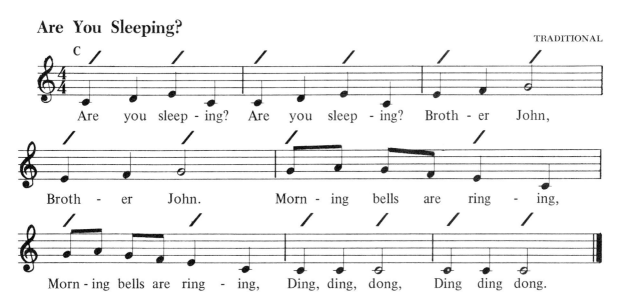

Other one chord songs:

My Goose, Thy Goose
Row, Row, Row Your Boat
Scotland's Burning
There's a Hole in My Bucket

Two Chord Song

Skip to My Lou

Try to sing these other two chord songs and let your ear tell you where to change the chords.

Bow, Bow, Belinda	G Major
Farmer in the Dell	F Major
Go Tell Aunt Rhody	F Major
Hokey Pokey	G Major
Hush Little Baby	F Major
He's Got the Whole World	C Major
Kookaburra	F Major
Looby Loo	C Major
Paw-Paw-Patch	G Major
Polly Wolly Doodle	G Major
Six Little Ducks	F Major

Three Chord Song

Jimmie Crack Corn

Try these other three chord songs and let your ear tell you where to change the chords.

Happy Birthday	F Major
Home on the Range	F Major
O Susanna	F Major
Old MacDonald Had a Farm	F Major
This Land is Your Land	F Major
This Old Man	F Major
Jingle Bells	F Major
Silent Night	C Major
Marines Hymn	C Major
Red River Valley	F Major

Songs in the Minor Mode

Joshua Fit the Battle of Jericho

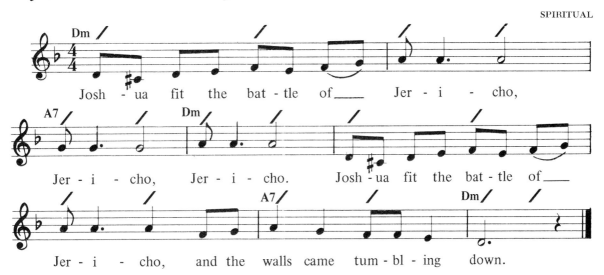

Zum Gali Gali

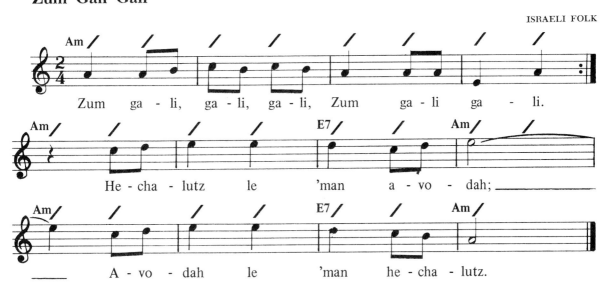

Wayfaring Stranger	d minor
God Rest Ye Merry Gentlemen	d minor
Zum Gali Gali	a minor
When Johnny Comes Marching Home	a minor
O Come, O Come Emmanuel	d minor
What Child Is This	d minor

THE UKULELE AND FOLK GUITAR

Both the ukulele and guitar are ideal instruments for recreational use. In fact, they are probably the most popular instruments for this purpose. They are both fretted instruments, and reinforce the vocal line harmonically without distracting from the audible quality of the vocal tone. The rhythmic effect of strumming helps to maintain the cohesion of the singing group. One player is adequate for small groups, but there may be several players accompanying larger groups.

The ukulele is the easiest of the two instruments to tune and play. It has only four strings, while the guitar has six. The uke is tuned by tightening or loosening the pegs until the pitch corresponds with the pitches G, C, E, A on the piano or tuning pipe. (See diagram on page 70.) The 'G" string is the one closest to the chin when holding the instrument in a traditional position. Some teachers use a simple song-pattern, such as "My dog has fleas" on the tuning pitches as a preliminary experience. It tends to reinforce the pitches of the strings "by ear."

The finger patterns for playing the ukulele are shown on page 70. The beginning problems arise from changing finger positions rapidly enough to maintain the rhythmic flow of the music. It is usual to begin with simple two-chord melodies before advancing to three chords or more.

The guitar is a versatile instrument capable of producing rich sounds. It has six strings tuned to the pitches E, A, D, G, B, and E. (See diagram on page 71.) Strumming patterns and chord symbols accompany many contemporary recreational song collections.

The following song indicates an alternating change between the I and V^7 chords. The symbols are given in the key of C. An even three-beat strum is appropriate for this song. The beat should be kept steady and the chords should move smoothly from one to the other.

"The More We Get Together"

Traditional

Uke:

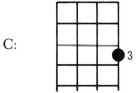

C:

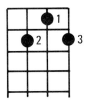

G⁷:

Strum on each beat
of the measure:

	C	C	G⁷	C
3/4 The	more we get to	gether, to	gether, to	gether,
The	more we get to	gether the	happier we'll	be.

	G⁷	C	G⁷	C
For	your friends are	my friends, and	my friends are	your friends.

	C	C	G⁷	C
The	more we get to	gether the	happier we'll	be.

The following song contains the two chords of C and G⁷ for the guitar. The symbols are given in the key of C. Strum on the first beat of each measure where the chord symbols are indicated. The beats should be kept steady and the chords should move smoothly from one to the other.

"O, Dear What Can the Matter Be?"

Traditional

Guitar:

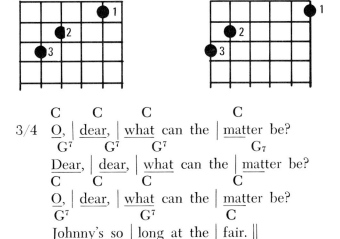

Strum on 1st beat
of the measure:

	C	C	C	C
3/4	O,	dear,	what can the	matter be?

	G⁷	G⁷	G⁷	G₇
	Dear,	dear,	what can the	matter be?

	C	C	C	C
	O,	dear,	what can the	matter be?

	G⁷	G⁷	C
	Johnny's so	long at the	fair. ||

Additional songs to practice uke and guitar chords in the key of C.

Joy to the World

ISAAC WATTS

LOWELL MASON

1. Joy to the world! the Lord is come; Let

earth re - ceive her King; _____ Let

ev - 'ry __ heart __ pre - pare __ Him __ room, _____ And

heav'n and na - ture __ sing, And __ heav'n and na - ture __ sing, And __

heav'n __ and heav'n _____ and na - ture sing.

My Hat

(MEIN HUT)

GERMANY

My hat it has three cor - ners; _____ Three

cor - ners has my hat; _____ And

had it not three cor - ners, _____ Then

it is not my hat. _____

Mein Hut er hat drei Ecken;
Drei Ecken hat mein Hut;
Und hat er nicht drei Ecken;
Denn das ist nicht mein Hut.

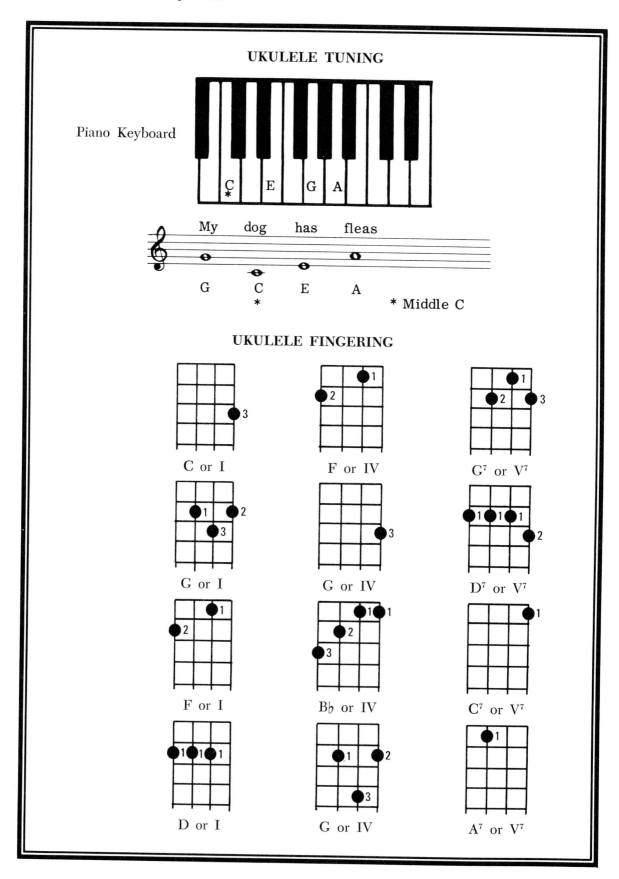

UKULELE TUNING

Piano Keyboard

My dog has fleas

* Middle C

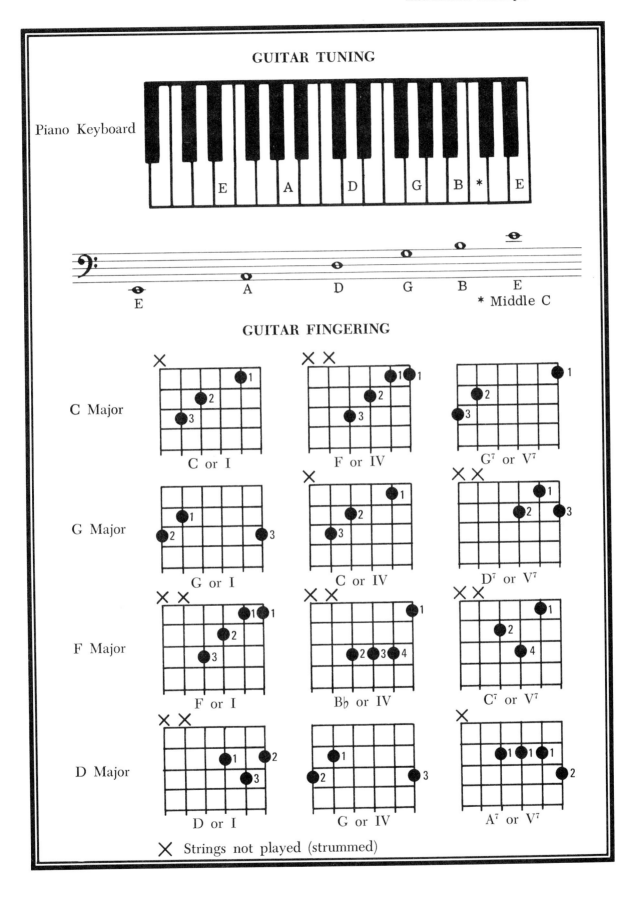

PIANO CHORDING

Simple piano chording can be a great asset to music leaders in a recreational program. Besides playing melody and harmony in a traditional way, the leader can often conduct with the right hand as he plays chords rhythmically with the left. For these purposes, the finger positions of three basic chords (I, IV, and V⁷) in a few keys can be easily mastered.

Each chord consists of three pitches sounded simultaneously. Each chord relates harmonically to the melodic line. The "formula" for moving from a I chord, (tonic) to a V⁷ chord (dominant-seventh) in every major key is the same. The numbers in the formula below represent the degrees of the scale.

5 (so) ←————→ 5 (so)
        same

3 (mi)‾up ½ step ————→ 4 (fa)

1 (do)‾
     down ————→ 7 (ti)
     ½ step

The formula for moving from the I chord (tonic) to the IV chord (sub-dominant) is:

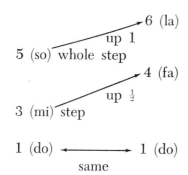

                 → 6 (la)
5 (so)‾up 1 whole step

                 → 4 (fa)
3 (mi)‾up ½ step

1 (do) ←————→ 1 (do)
       same

The formula for moving from the IV chord (sub-dominant) to the V⁷ chord (dominant-seventh) is:

6 (la)‾down 1
          whole step
          → 5 (so)

4 (fa) ←————→ 4 (fa)
      same

1 (do)‾
     down ————→ 7 (ti)
     ½ step

In staff notation, the chords in the progression, I-IV-V⁷-I, are given below in both treble and bass clefs. These should become automatic as you sing and play the following.

Piano Chords
(Key of C)

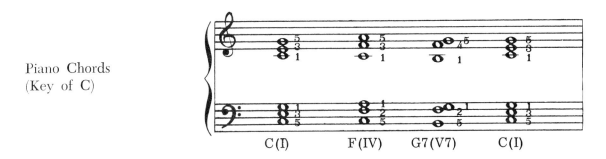

C (I)   F (IV)   G7 (V7)   C (I)

Jack and Jill

MOTHER GOOSE RHYME   J. W. ELLIOTT

1. Jack   and   Jill   went   up   the   hill   to   fetch   a   pail   of   wa - ter;   Jack   fell   down   and   broke   his   crown,   And   Jill   came tum - bling   af - ter.

2. Up Jack got, and home he ran as fast as he could caper,
    There his mother bound his head with vinegar and brown paper.

Piano Chords
(Key of F)

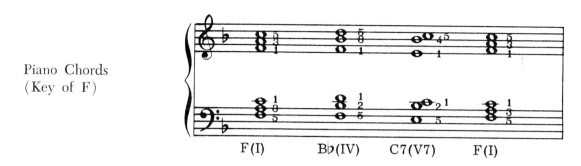

F(I)   Bb(IV)   C7(V7)   F(I)

He's Got the Whole World in His Hands

SPIRITUAL

1. He's got the whole world— in His hands,— He's got the

whole world— in His hands,— He's got the whole world—

in His hands,— He's got the whole world in His hands.

2. He's got the wind and rain in His hands.
3. He's got that little baby in His hands.
4. He's got you and me in His hands.
5. He's got everybody in His hands.
6. He's got the whole world in His hands.

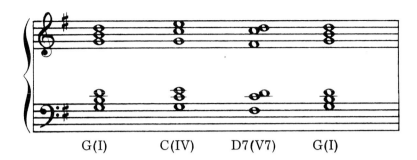

Piano Chords
(Key of G)

G(I)   C(IV)   D7(V7)   G(I)

The Old Brass Wagon

Square dance

MIDWESTERN U. S.

1. Circle to the left, the old brass wag - on, Circle to the left, the old brass wag - on, Cir-cle to the left, the old brass wag - on, You're the one my dar - ling.

2. Circle to the right, the old brass wagon, etc.
3. Swing, oh swing, the old brass wagon, etc.
4. Promenade around, the old brass wagon, etc.
5. Swing your partner, the old brass wagon, etc.
6. Break and swing, the old brass wagon, etc.
7. Promenade in, the old brass wagon, etc.

TEXTS OF MORE FAMILIAR SONGS TO SING AND PLAY

The following songs can be accompanied in any major key which is in a comfortable range for the singers.

DOWN IN THE VALLEY

Kentucky Folk Song

F Major   I V^7
Meter   Down in the valley, the valley so low,
9   V^7 I
8   Hang your head over, hear the winds blow.
                 I V^7
Hear the winds blow, dear, hear the winds blow,
           V^7 I
Hang your head over, hear the winds blow.

Clementine

F Major	I	I	I	V⁷

Meter 3
4

In a cavern, in a canyon, excavating for a mine,

        V⁷   I   V⁷   I

Dwelt a miner, forty-niner, and his daughter Clementine.

      I   I   I   V⁷

Oh my darling, Oh my darling, Oh my darling Clementine.

      V⁷   I   V⁷   I

You are lost and gone forever, dreadful sorry, Clementine.

Looby Loo

C Major	I	I	I	V⁷

Meter 2
4

Here we go looby loo, Here we go looby light,

I   I V⁷   I

Here we go looby loo, all on a Saturday night.

London Bridge

C Major — I, I, V⁷, I

Meter 2/4

London bridge is falling down, falling down, falling down,

I, I, V⁷, I

London bridge is falling down, my fair lady.

Kum Ba Yah

C Major — I, IV, I

Meter 3/4

Kum ba yah, my Lord, Kum ba yah,

I, I, V⁷

Kum ba yah, my Lord, Kum ba yah,

I, IV, I

Kum ba yah, my Lord, Kum ba yah,

V⁷ I, V⁷, I

O Lord————Kum ba yah.

Rocka My Soul

Spiritual

C Major — I

Meter 4/4

Rocka my soul, in the bosom of Abraham

V⁷

Rocka my soul, in the bosom of Abraham

I

Rocka my soul, in the bosom of Abraham

V⁷ I

(clap) Oh, rocka my soul.

THE MORE WE GET TOGETHER

F Major	I	V⁷ I

F Major   I   V⁷   I

Meter   The more we get together, together, together

3   I   I   V⁷   I

4   The more we get together, the happier we'll be.

        V⁷   I   V⁷   I

For your friends are my friends and my friends are your friends.

        I   I   V⁷   I

The more we get together, the happier we'll be.

SILENT NIGHT

C Major   I   I

Meter   Silent night! Holy night!

6   V⁷   I

8   All is calm, all is bright

      IV   I

Round yon virgin mother and child!

      IV   I

Holy infant, so tender and mild,

V⁷   I

Sleep in heavenly peace,

  I   V⁷   I

Sleep in heavenly peace,

YANKEE DOODLE

F Major   I   V⁷   I   V⁷

Meter   Father and I went down to camp along with Captain Goodin,

2   I   IV   V⁷   I

4   And there we saw the men and boys as thick as hasty puddin';

     IV   I

Yankee doodle, keep it up, Yankee doodle dandy,

     IV   V⁷   I

Mind the music and the step and with the girls be handy.

MICHAEL ROW THE BOAT ASHORE

C Major   I   I   IV I

Meter   1. Michael row the boat ashore, Allelujah

4   I   V⁷   V⁷ I

4   Michael row the boat ashore, Allelujah

    2. The river is wide and the water is deep, Allelujah (repeat).

    3. Sister, help to trim the sail, Allelujah (repeat).

CHORDING WITH RESONATOR BELLS

The use of resonator bells of the individual type can provide a simple and satisfying chording experience. Chording accompaniments to simple songs can be well-played and musically sensitive with the practice of striking techniques and steady rhythmic playing. In the songs which follow individual persons should each play the bell represented by the appropriate letter name indicated above the melody. It is usually well to sing along and listen carefully as the chords change.

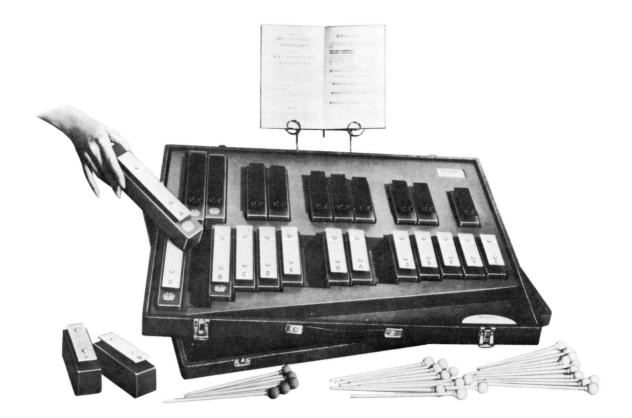

Sandy Land

1. Make my liv-ing in sand-y land, Make my liv-ing in sand-y land,

Make my liv-ing in sand-y land, La-dies, fare you well.

Ring, Ring the Banjo

1. The time is nev-er drear-y if a fel-low nev-er
come a-gain Su - san-na, by the gas-light of the

groans; The la - dies nev - er wea - ry with the
moon, We'll strum the old pi - an - o when the

Ring, Ring the Banjo

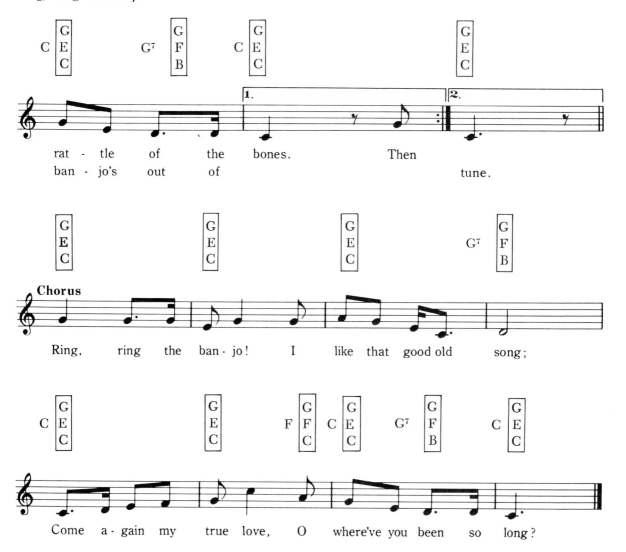

rat - tle of the bones. Then
ban - jo's out of tune.

Chorus

Ring, ring the ban - jo! I like that good old song;

Come a - gain my true love, O where've you been so long?

2. Oh, never count the bubbles when there's water in the spring,
   There's no one who has trouble when he has this song to sing,
   The beauties of creation will never lose their charm
   While I roam the old plantation with my true love on my arm.

3. My love, I'll have to leave you while the river's runing high,
   But I will not deceive you, so don't you wipe your eye,
   I'm going to make some money, but I'll come another day,
   I'll come again, my honey, if I have to work my way.

Drunken Sailor

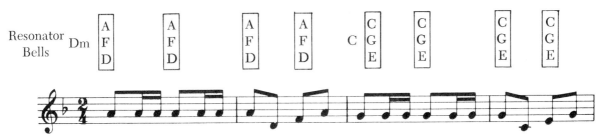

1. What shall we do with a drunk-en sai-or, What shall we do with a drunk-en sail-or,

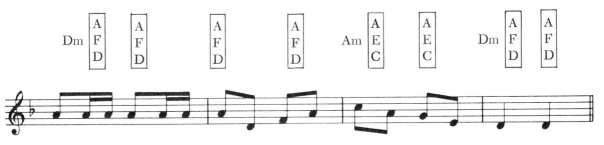

What shall we do with a drunk-en sail - or, Ear-ly in the morn - ing?

Chorus

Hoo - ray and up she ris - es, Hoo - ray and up she ris - es,

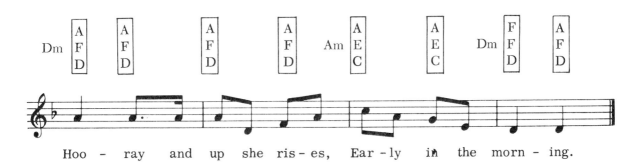

Hoo - ray and up she ris - es, Ear-ly in the morn - ing.

2. Put him in the longboat until he's sober, (etc.)
3. Pull out the plug and wet him all over, (etc.)
4. Heave him by the leg in a running bowline.° (etc.)
5. Put him in the scuppers°° with a hose-pipe on him, (etc.)
6. Toss him in the brig until he's sober, (etc.)

°Rope to keep sail taut.
°°Opening in ship's side for water run off.

SIMPLE "ROCK" PROGRESSIONS

Besides learning simple traditional chords for diatonic folk songs, young people today are very familiar with the musical patterns in "Rock" music. The following rhythmic, harmonic, and melodic progressions will add an element of interest to a jam session.

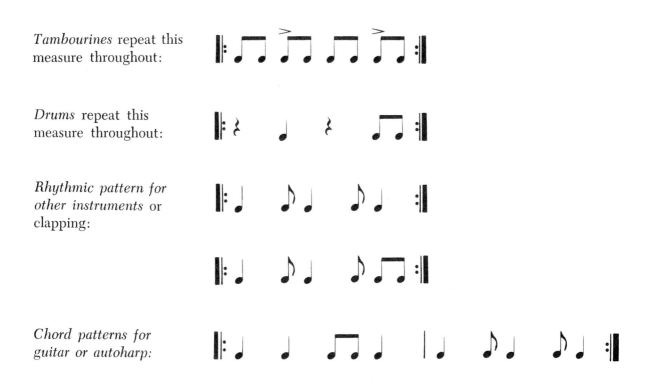

(each block represents one measure of piano patterns)

C⁷	C⁷	C⁷	C⁷	F⁷	F⁷	F⁷	F⁷	C⁷	C⁷	C⁷	C⁷

G⁷	G⁷	G⁷	G⁷	C⁷	C⁷	C⁷	C⁷

Melodic Patterns for Piano:

As arranged by a graduate class in music education at the University of Michigan, Ann Arbor, Michigan.

SELECTED REFERENCES

1. BALL, ERNIE. *How to Play the Guitar.* New York: Ernie Ball, Inc., 1979.
2. BAY, MEL. *Modern Guitar.* Mel Bay Publications, Inc., 1975.
3. d'AUBERGE, ALFRED. *Alfred's Basic Guitar Method.* Sherman Oaks, California: Alfred Music Company, Inc.
4. JOHN, ROBERT W. and CHARLES H. DOUGLAS. *Playing Social and Recreational Instruments.* Englewood Cliffs: N. J.: Prentice-Hall Inc., 1972.
5. NYE, ROBERT E. and MEG PETERSON. *Teaching Music with the Autoharp.* Union, N. J.: Music Education Group, 1973.
6. PETERSON, MEG. *The Many Ways to Play the Autoharp,* 2 vols. Union, N. J.: Oscar Schmidt-International Inc., 1966.
7. WHEELER, LAWRENCE and LOIS RAEBECK. *Orff and Kodaly Adapted for the Elementary School.* Dubuque, Iowa: Wm. C. Brown Co., 1972.

11.

sound exploration

Exploring and organizing sounds into expressive musical entities is suitable for recreational activities, especially with young people. It is a constant and readily available means for self- and group-initiated experiences. These are highly motivating because they require originality and creation.[1]

The most accessible sounds are those we can produce ourselves, such as singing, humming, and whistling. These are called "self-sounds." With a little thought and experimentation, numerous self-sounds are possible: moaning, hissing, pouring, cackling, gasping, murmuring, sighing, sniffing, clicking, etc. The effect of each of these can be altered by variation of pitch, dynamics, and tempo. Other ways of producing self-sounds with parts of the body are by clapping, stamping, clicking fingers, and slapping knees.

In addition, the sounds in the environment, whether indoors or out, provide unending sources for a variety of sounds in creative activities—classroom sounds; sounds in the home; sounds of objects or machinery; sounds of nature; various speeds of tape recorded sounds. All of these are open-ended sources for composition and creativity.

Standard musical instruments provide additional media for creative purposes. These instruments, including the piano, may be played in many ways through experimentation so that sounds can be summoned other than those generally associated with the instrument. Original instruments made by students themselves are also effective and should be incorporated into compositional experiences.

For many recreational purposes, such as playgrounds and community centers, group compositional projects are sources of satisfaction. Teams may work simultaneously on a given sound problem. Leaders and group organization should remain flexible. It is often best to begin with a simple project before proceeding to more extended pieces. An example of a simple team project might be: create a fifteen-second piece which uses only two instruments of different registers (high, low). Select one instrument to maintain a repeated rhythmic pattern (*ostinato*) throughout.

Sources for inspiration in creative composition may also include dramatic ideas such as events, poems, or commercials. Mood music can be created to enrich a story, or as "atmosphere" for various holidays.

---

1. Several of the creative ideas in this section are taken from *Music Bulletin # 1: Classroom Composition: An Approach to Music Learnings* by Eugene W. Troth (Cincinnati, Ohio: American Book Company, 1970). Used by permission.

Before the groups divide for their compositional work, they may need suggestions on a procedure for their group work, such as the following:

1. Read the project assignment together as a group.
2. Discuss the possibilities for sounds to express your project.
3. Experiment until you find the sounds with which you are satisfied.
4. Decide the order in which the sounds will be organized. (Don't neglect the possibility for spontaneity or improvisation where appropriate.)
5. Perform your composition and continue to listen critically. Ask: Does the piece have a good beginning and ending? Does it have interest? Does it have variety? Do we like it? How could it be changed, improved, refined?

The following series of composition projects may serve as illustrations of the unlimited possibilities within this area. These should be limited to 1-3 minutes each.

Project 1:
Goal: Create a musical abstraction of a haunted house.
Sounds: 1 vocal sound, 2 instrumental sounds, 1 spoken word, 1 body sound
Limitations: Contrasts should be obvious. Use slow-fast-slow pattern for tempo.

Project 2:
Goal: Create a musical mood piece for the words: "Let the Sunshine In."
Sounds: 1 autoharp, 3 other classroom instruments, 1 vocal sound
Limitations: Start slowly and softly and gradually increase both dynamics and tempo.

Project 3:
Goal: Create a musical "picture" of the following text:

> Praise ye the god of gold;
> Praise ye the god of silver;
> Praise ye the god of wood;
> Praise ye the god of stone;
> Praise ye the god of brass;
> Praise ye the gods;

Sounds: 4 instruments, 1 vocal sound
Limitations: Use the dynamics level of loud-soft-loud as an overall pattern; start with one instrument.

Project 4:
Goal: Create a musical "Picture" of the poem below.
Sounds: 1 body sound, 1 vocal sound, 3 instruments
Limitations: Begin with one sound, adding others one at a time

> Slowly slowly the drip drip drip
> Splick splick . . . splock of coming rain
> And then the roar
> As icily cold needles penetrate the skin of things
> To the very very bone core.[2]
> . . . Jennifer Lloyd

2. From *The Wind and the Rain*. Collected by Richard Lewish with photographs by Helen Buttfield. New York: Simon and Schuster, Inc., 1968, p. 18.

Project 5:

Goal: Create a musical description of the "feeling" sense (tactile) of the objects given you. (Suggestions: cotton, pine cone, aluminum foil.)

Sounds: 3 classroom instruments, 2 vocal sounds

Limitations: Begin and end with the softest sound you use in your composition.

Project 6:

Goal: Create a musical fabric using the following words as inspiration: "snap, crackle, pop."

Sounds: 2 homemade sounds, 1 instrumental sound.

Limitations: The sounds must always be presented in the word order above; sounds may overlap and variety may be gained by tempo and dynamics.

Project 7:

Goal: Create a sound description of the mood of "Christmas is here."

Sounds: Bells, 2 body sounds, 1 classroom instrument.

Limitations: The piece must have three sections alternating somehow from loud-soft-loud.

Project 8:

Goal: Create a sound study based on the life of an astronaut."

Sounds: 2 classroom instruments, 2 body sounds, 1 vocal sound.

Limitations: Start with many sounds together and gradually diminish into silence.

Project 9:

Goal: Create a sound description of a nature walk entitled: "Alone with God."

Sounds: Self-sounds only.

Limitations: "Silences" within the composition will be obvious.

SCIENCE AND SOUND

Many experiences relate sound with scientific principles. The following lesson outline demonstrates the concept of wind-instrument sound production.

Materials:
1. Eight *no-return* pop bottles
2. Funnel
3. Bucket of water
4. Cup
5. Mallet
6. Food coloring

Objectives:
1. Recognition and creation of a diatonic scale.
2. Pitch discrimination.
3. Understanding of the scientific aspects of pitch.
4. Ability to apply a scale in the student's own composition.
5. Recognition of melodic direction.

Procedures:

1. Place the empty bottles on a table at random. Ask the class, "How can we make an instrument from these bottles?" Some possible answers are: Fill the bottles to different levels and either strike the bottles or blow into them.
2. Take a couple of bottle and fill some of them with varying levels of water. First strike the bottles then blow into them. The pitch will be opposite, in other words, the empty bottle will be the highest pitch when struck and the lowest pitch when blown into. Ask the students why this is so. If they do not know then ask them what is vibrating to make the sound. Then discuss length of the vibrating source in relation to the pitch. (This could launch into a discussion of other instruments and their sound sources.)
3. Many instruments have enough selections of pitch to create a scale. How could we create a scale on these botttles? By putting different levels of water in them. Use the blower end of a vacuum cleaner as a constant source of air. Have a student regulate the vacuum, another student filling the bottles and the class determining whether the tones are sharp or flat and how to correct them.

Possible Uses and Lessons for this Creation:

1. Listen to songs with a diatonic scale in them: "Joy to the World," "Do-Re-Mi" from the *Sounds of Music* etc.
2. Students can create an *ostinato* on the bottles to a song they know.
3. Students can create their own composition with the bottles. (It would also be very easy for them to practice at home.)
4. Students can make two or more sets of bottle scales for harmony. (This could be related to a pipe organ.)
5. From this creation it would be easy to transfer the sounds to the staff.
6. From this, a unit on instrumental sound source and the basic principles of vibration and pitch could be presented.

SELECTED REFERENCES

1. CROOK, ELIZABETH, et al. *Silver Burdett Music,* "Working With Sounds," levels 5 and 6, and "Sound; the Raw Material of Music," levels 7 and 8. Morristown, N. J.: Silver Burdett Company, 1974-5, 1981.
2. ELLIOTT, DOROTHY GAIL. "Junk Music," *Music Educators Journal* 58, 5 (January 1972); pp. 58-59.
3. HOENACK, PEG. "Unleash Creativity—Let Them Improvise!" 57, 9 (May, 1971), pp. 33-35.
4. MARSH, MARY VAL, et al. *Spectrum of Music,* "Sources of Musical Sounds" and "Electronic Music." New York: The Macmillan Company, 1975.
5. MARSH, MARY VAL. *Explore and Discover Music.* New York: The Macmillan Company, 1970.
6. MEHR, NORMA. "Improvising with Resonator Bells," *Music Educators Journal,* 63, 1 (September 1976), p. 84.
7. PALMER, MARY. *Sound Exploration and Discovery.* New York: The Center for Applied Research in Education. 1974.
8. PAYNTER, JOHN and PETER ASTON. *Sound and Silence.* Cambridge, England: University Press, 1970.
9. SCHAFER, R. MURRAY. *Creative Music Education.* New York: Schirmer Books, 1976.

12.

choral speaking

Choral speaking includes a wide variety of stimulating and expressive activities for recreational use. By defintion, it is the organization of spoken words into meaningful patterns. Choral speaking is similar to singing, except that a speaking voice is substituted for a singing tone. Exciting and artistic effects may thus be achieved. This is especially true when spoken words and word-groupings are combined with musical or self-sounds.[1]

Choral speaking groups are especially suitable to recreational settings because they allow for involvement by persons of any age. These may be in single age groups or in combined groups of different ages. The high, light registers of children's voices are often combined with the qualities and ranges of adult voices.

The size of choral speaking groups depends on the practice aspects of the recreational situation. All who are interested should somehow be accommodated. In this sense, the basic goal of recreation, which is pleasure and enjoyment, will have been taken into consideration. However, when selection is made for other reasons, it is usual to have twelve or more persons in a group. Less than twelve limits the possibilities for fullness and variety.

Effective choral speaking depends upon the appropriate classification of the voices themselves.[2] Each member of the group should be heard individually and placed in either the light, medium, or dark category. For this purpose, the leader directs each person to speak a phrase, such as: "Hello, everybody. One two, three, four, five" in a normal, natural speaking voice. All members of the group should be called upon to assist in voice description and classification. This procedure emphasizes the importance of attentive listening, which is prerequisite to good choral speaking. It also tends to create a "game" spirit and the feeling of group dependency.

As soon as individuals are classified, they should be seated in groups. The physical arrangement or placement is not important except in the context of the composition being performed. Once in classified groups, each group should recite the "testing" phrase in turn. Interest is immmediately aroused as all witness the results of spoken group "color."

Choral speaking material for both informal occasions and public performance is only limited by the imagination of those involved. Compositions may range from a brief rendition of the local news to an epic poem. In the beginning, however, it is best to begin with simple word patterns and sound combinations which can be enriched by the use of dynamic levels, accents, and rhythmic manipulation.

---

1. See p. 71 for a description and listing of self-sounds.
2. The ability to "carry a tune" does not necessarily affect voice classification in a speaking group.

The following is an illustration of a choral speaking presentation using a newspaper weather report. Instruments and/or sound effects may be added for variety and expressive power.

WEATHER REPORT   By J. B. and S. M.

Weather Report: Monday will be fair and warmer with a few scattered showers toward evening. Lowered temperatures expected Tuesday with a ten percent chance of snow.

Choral Speaking

Enter all voices (very low in strict rhythm): Monday will be fair, Monday will be fair, Monday will be fair.

Enter solo light voice (little child quality): Monday will be warmer and warmer and warmer.

Enter medium voices (raucously in loud voice): scattered showers toward evening (pause).

Enter all voices (moderately): Monday will be. . .

Enter light voices (loud): fair and warm. . .

Enter heavy voices (louder): with scattered showers toward evening (pause).

Enter medium and light voices sustaining the vowel sound "Ooooo" throughout the following entrance.

Enter heavy voices (dirge-like): lowered temperatures expected Tuesday, lowered temperatures expected Tuesday.

Enter light voices (fast and shrill): with a ten percent chance of snow.

Enter all voices (loud, gradually diminishing): ohhhhh.

More extended compositions can be created using the names of cities or counties. These may take on fun and interest when local states are used. The following is an example from South Carolina.

SOUTH CAROLINA!   By J. B. and S. M.

Enter light voices (fast and soft): Lancaster, Beaufort and Pawleys Island

Enter medium voices (same tempo a little louder): Orangeburg, Camden and Aiken

Enter light voices (very slowly): Greenwood, Spartanburg, Walterboro

Enter heavy voices (whispered): St. Matthews, St. George, Bishopville

Enter light voices, medium and loud voices (in rapid succession, very loud): Columbia!!

Enter solo medium voice: Bamberg

Enter solo heavy voice: Bennettsville (in rapid succession)

Enter solo light voice: Batesburg

Enter light voices (chant softly and gradually increase in volume):

CHARLESTON (During this chant, the medium voices speak deliberately): Myrtle Beach, Marion Mullins, McCormick

Enter solo light voice (piercingly): Killian!!

Enter heavy voices chanting: Columbia as medium voices and light voices chant: Charleston. Both groups gradually increase speed and volume until a frenetic effect is reached ending abruptly with a very loud cymbal crash.

Short poems, sometimes created by the groups themselves, are effective for fast-pace renditions in choral speaking. The following is an example.

LAMENT By J. B.

Heavy voices: I hate to say goodbye to you;
Medium voices: It's such a stupid thing to do.
Light voices: For we have barely said hello;
All voices: And now you have to up and go!

There are many poems.and readings that lend themselves to total group involvement. The following two poems by Sharon Webb Hutchison would be examples of this type. Try to arrange the parts to allow for variety in tone quality and dynamics in order to bring out the meaning of the texts.

I DIDN'T SLEEP A WINK By Sharon Webb Hutchison (Used by permission.)

I didn't sleep a wink last night
'Cause snakes were under my bed,
While flapping bats and flying squirrels
Were circling overhead.

And hiding in the closet
Was a great big hungry bear,
And lurking in the shadows
Was a lion in his lair.

The gorilla in the curtain
Was eyeing me for lunch,
And the leopard on the dresser
Thought that I'd be great to munch!

A six-foot alligator
Was crawling on the floor,
And worst of all, the boogey-man
Was coming through the door!

But my dad was right behind him,
"I love you," he would say,
As he turned and flicked the light on,
And sent them all away.

SALLY ANN PEARL By Sharon Webb Hutchison (Used by permission.)

"I want to play the tuba,"
Said Sally Ann Pearl.
"But you can't," said her mother,
"For you're a little girl."

"Well then "I'll play the trombone
With its long slick slide,"
But her Daddy said "No!"
So she slipped away and cried.

"I really like the drum
With its rat-a-tat-tat."
But they thought of all the noise,
And that ended that!

"Then what about the saxophone
Or bass violin?"
But they each shook their head
And they wouldn't give in.

"Well then what can I play?"
Cried an angry Sally Ann.
Said her mother,
"The piano and the harp are grand!"

And her father said,
"The flute and violin are swell,
Or the piccolo, the cello,
Or a set of tiny bells."

"But I don't like those instruments
As much as all the others,"
Which was baffling to her dad
And confusing to her mother.

"In an age of women's freedom
I demand the equal right,
To select and choose an instrument
and play with all my might."

Her Daddy shrugged his shoulders,
Her mother gave a grin,
Then both looked straight
   at Sally Ann,
And said, "O.K., you win!"

And that is why in Elmwood
At the district band fair
You will find a female tuba player
Sitting first chair.

There are many ways to combine choral speaking with music: 1. Recorded musical backgrounds may be added to intensify the dramatic effects of the spoken word; 2. Rhythmic effects may be produced on various percussion instruments; and 3. Different combinations of the spoken word with singing may be arranged. The following is an example of such a combination.

Divide the group into two sections and seat them all in a large semicircle with the director in the middle facing them. Begin the presentation by having the entire group sing "There Are Birds of Every Plume" in unison. Next, have each person think of a different bird

There Are Birds of Every Plume

JMB

and speak its name when the director points to that person. Interesting and creative effects can be achieved as the director changes tempi, and alters speech levels and dynamics. After approximately a minute and a half of this, each persons in one section is to perform bird sounds in any oral fashion (whistle, tongue-clucking, hissing, vocalizing). Then, bring in the second section doing the same thing. The sections can alternate until the desired effect is reached. Finally, the presentation is concluded with the entire group singing the sound in round form as indicated very softly.

This format can be followed by incorporating singing, speech and sound effects with any familiar round. Suggestions are:

ROUND	SPEECH	SOUND EFFECTS
"Row, Row, Row, Your Boat"	Names of various types of boats	Any sounds relating nautical things
"Three Blind Mice"	Names of various animals	Animal sounds
"French Cathedrals"	Names of different famous cathedrals	Vocalize the sounds of bells.
"Are You Sleeping"	Phrases relative to sleep (Good night, Sleep tight, Pleasant dreams, etc.)	Sounds relating to sleep

SELECTED REFERENCES

1. BETTENBENDER, JOHN, ed. *Poetry Festival*. New York: Dell Publishing Co., 1966.
2. *Japanese Haiku*. Mt. Vernon, N. Y.: The Peter Pauper Press, 1955.
3. LATHEM, EDWARD COUNERY. *The Poetry of Robert Frost*. New York: Holt, Rinehart and Winston, Inc. 1969.
4. NASH, GRACE. *Verses and Movement*. Chicago: Kitchuig (Educational Division of Ludwig Press), 1967.
5. POVERMIRE, E. KINGSLEY. *Choral Speaking and the Verse Choir*. New York: A. S. Barnes, 1975.
6. SILVERSTEIN, SHEL. *Where the Sidewalk Ends*. New York: Harper & Row, 1974.
7. REGNIERS, BEATRICE et al. *Poems Children Sit Still For*. New York: Scholastic Book Services, 1973.

13.

dramatic movement and traditional dancing

Dramatic movement is one type of rhythmic response that lends itself very well to recreational activities. It provides a means for improvisation, mime, storytelling, musical response, and accompaniment. Ideas for dramatized movement range from everyday experiences, such as a simple gesture or greeting, to a dramatized composition based on a poem or painting.[1] The subject chosen will naturally depend upon the age and interest of the participants.

Probably the most frequent starting point for dramatic movement is pantomime. Simple gestures or ideas are translated into motion and then extended to express a total concept—no matter how small or short. Familiar gestures, or actions which may be translated into pantomime are: shaking hands, waving, winking, eating, sleeping, crying, laughing, praying, applauding. These may be expanded by transferring the movement to another part of the body, changing the rhythm of the gesture, increasing or diminishing the size of the movement, or adding other body parts to the movement. Step patterns may also be added to expand the total action as follows:

Shake Hands:

1. Turn to someone near you and shake right hands, left hands.
2. Take this person as your partner; everyone form a circle.
3. Face your partner and shake right hands again. Walk around the circle shaking hands alternately right and left with each person you meet. (Half of the children will move clockwise and half counter-clockwise as in a grand right and left.)
4. Do the same thing, substituting a polka for a walk.
5. Do it again. Extend your hand, but don't touch anyone.

The senses of touch, taste, and smell are wonderful sources for dramatic movement. The following group activity involves the sense of touch.

---

1. Several illustrated lessons for dramatized movement may be found in *Rhythm in Music and Dance for Children* by Sally Monsour, Marilyn Cohen and Patricia Lindell © 1966 by Wadsworth Publishing Company, Belmont, California 94002. "What do you Feel?" and "The Machine" are taken directly from this book reprinted with permission of the publisher.

What Do You Feel

Thoughts to Teach By

Choose objects having different shapes and textures.

Encourage children to devise their own movements, without imitating their classmates.

PROCEDURE	HINTS
1. Place items with different shapes and textures into separate paper bags.	Rough, hard, smooth, soft—corn cob, sandpaper, ice cube, velvet, fur, feathers.
2. Divide into groups. Give each group a bag containing a different item.	Direct them not to look inside.
3. Each person in the group reaches into the bag, one at a time to feel the contents.	The stimulus for movement should be entirely tactile.
4. Each person devises his own movement based on the texture of the object as he felt it.	If you do not wish to devote much time to the lesson, this part may be improvised, with steps 4 and 5 combined.
5. All in the same group perform together.	They should not attempt to produce organized group movement. However, individual movemens will probably be of a similar quality.
6. After the group performs, show the objects from which the movement has evolved.	This will clarify the exercise and satisfy the children's curiosity.

Games, sports, nature, animals, mass media, and the events surrounding mechanization and urban living are all excellent sources for groups to use in creating dramatized compositions, dances, and plays. Sounds are usually combined with extended dramatic ideas so that the composite can be very rewarding and often artistic. Involvement is at a high level if groups are allowed to initiate their own ideas. Giving little hints of ways to begin, material assistance, or help when things get "bogged" down, will naturally be the function of the leader or teacher. But, as far as possible, participants should explore most experiences on their own.

The project which follows illustrates a combined activity on mechanized movements entitled: "The Machine."[2] It includes dramatic idea, movement exploration, and sounds. It could also enrich concepts of rhythm reading.

The Machine

Write the chart below on the blackboard and refer to it throughout the lesson. If the group is unfamiliar with notation, omit that part of the chart and allow them to formulate their own rhythmic patterns, disregarding notation. Provide the conventional instruments listed on the chart, or simulated ones such as kitchen utensils, for group exploration and mechanical sounds and background in sound exploration.

Suggest that the group examine machines (ditto, typewriter, etc.) and improvise their own sound, patterns, and movements.

		RHYTHMIC PATTERNS	
SOUND	SUGGESTED MOVEMENT	YOUNGER GROUP	OLDER GROUP
Sand blocks	Horizontal lever—arm	$\frac{2}{4}$ ♩ ♩ | ♩ 𝄽 ‖	$\frac{5}{4}$ 𝅝 ♩ ♩ ♩ ‖

<hr>

2. Listen to selections such as "Steel Foundry," Mossolov Recording: Sounds of New Music, Folkways (FX 6160).

| | SUGGESTED MOVEMENT | RHYTHMIC PATTERNS | |
| SOUND | | YOUNGER GROUP | OLDER GROUP |

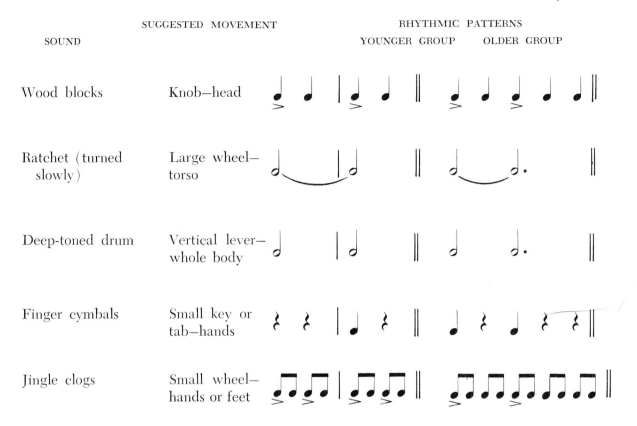

Wood blocks	Knob—head		
Ratchet (turned slowly)	Large wheel— torso		
Deep-toned drum	Vertical lever— whole body		
Finger cymbals	Small key or tab—hands		
Jingle clogs	Small wheel— hands or feet		

TRADITIONAL DANCE STEPS

There are many occasions in a recreation program when the basic patterns of traditional dance steps are needed. Although these are usually included in dance descriptions, they are not generally given in concise form in one place. It is with this in mind that the authors are including them here. The rhythm and dance references at the end of this section will often refer to several of these traditional steps[3] either as a part of the dance or as the basis for the entire dance.

Buzz Step (turning in place)

word cue		step	push	step	push
step pattern		R	L	R	L
rhythmic pattern	2/4				
underlying beat		—	—	—	—

---

3. Taken from *Rhythm in Music and Dance for Children,* Ibid., p. 79-80.

Jig

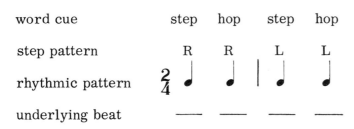

word cue	step	hop	step	hop
step pattern	R	R	L	L
rhythmic pattern				
underlying beat				

Mazurka

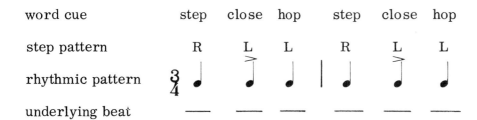

word cue	step	close	hop	step	close	hop
step pattern	R	L	L	R	L	L
rhythmic pattern						
underlying beat						

Pas de Basque

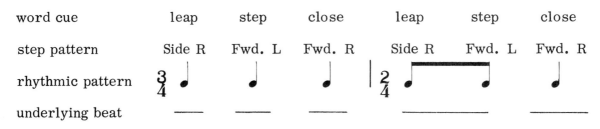

word cue	leap	step	close	leap	step	close
step pattern	Side R	Fwd. L	Fwd. R	Side R	Fwd. L	Fwd. R
rhythmic pattern						
underlying beat						

Polka

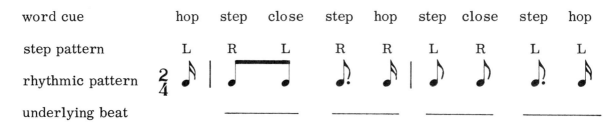

word cue	hop	step	close	step	hop	step	close	step	hop
step pattern	L	R	L	R	R	L	R	L	L
rhythmic pattern								
underlying beat								

Running Waltz

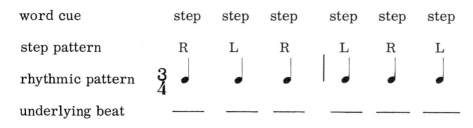

word cue	step	step	step	step	step	step
step pattern	R	L	R	L	R	L
rhythmic pattern						
underlying beat						

Schottische

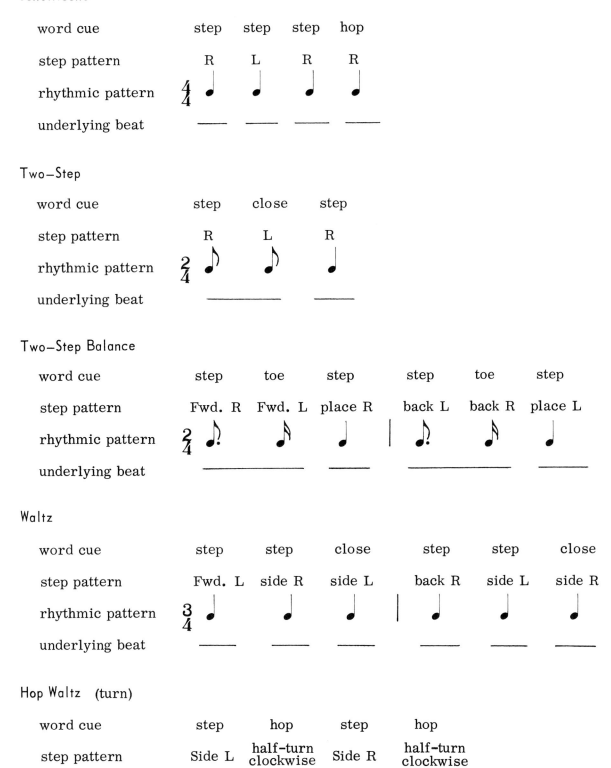

word cue	step	step	step	hop
step pattern	R	L	R	R

Two-Step

word cue	step	close	step
step pattern	R	L	R

Two-Step Balance

word cue	step	toe	step	step	toe	step
step pattern	Fwd. R	Fwd. L	place R	back L	back R	place L

Waltz

word cue	step	step	close	step	step	close
step pattern	Fwd. L	side R	side L	back R	side L	side R

Hop Waltz (turn)

word cue	step	hop	step	hop
step pattern	Side L	half-turn clockwise	Side R	half-turn clockwise

Waltz Balance

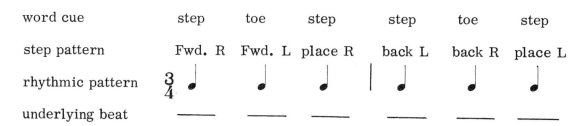

word cue		step	toe	step	step	toe	step
step pattern		Fwd. R	Fwd. L	place R	back L	back R	place L
rhythmic pattern	3/4	♩	♩	♩	♩	♩	♩
underlying beat		—	—	—	—	—	—

Two Middle Eastern Folk Dances: Hora and Dubka. Folk dancing in Mediterranean countries is usually done in groups which move in open circles or lines. There is a leader who determines any changes in direction or step pattern. The two dances below are similar in that the group forms a semi-circle with arms linked at shoulder level or hands held down at the sides. There should be little movement from the waist up and the entire torso should follow the movement direction of the feet.

It is important to maintain an informal group spirit of gaiety and fun when doing these dances. Once the basic beat pattern is felt by the group, leaders should be encouraged to create other step patterns as they go along.

The following songs represent typical tunes used with each dance. There are numerous folk dance recordings which can also be used. (See Appendix E for suggestions).

Hava Nagila

Hava Nagila

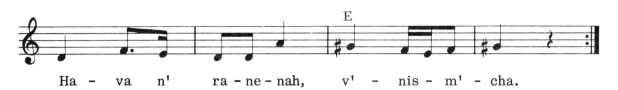

Ha - va n' ra - ne - nah, v' - nis - m' - cha.

U - ru, U - ru a - chim, U - ru a - chim b' -

lev sa - mey - ach, U - ru a - chim b' lev sa - mey - ach, U - ru a - chim b'

lev sa - mey - ach U - ru a - chim b' - lev sa - mey - ach

U - ru a - chim, U - ru a - chim b'lev sa - mey - ach.

Dance Directions: 8-Beat Hora (Israeli)

Beat:	1	2	3	4	5	6	7	8
Foot:	R	L	R	R	L	L	L	L
Movement:	Step to R	Step to R behind R	Step to R	Hop	Step to L	Step to L behind L	Step to L	Hop

Ala Da'lona

A - la da' lo - na A - la da' lo - na

hi - war shi - ma - li gha - yar ih - lo - na

ma - ba - di i - mi ma - ba - di ba - yi

ba - di ha - bi - bi as - mar ih - lo - na.

Fair Da'lona with dark skin   leave my mother and father
Chilled by the wind; I would   to visit my fair Da'lona.

Dance Directions: 6-beat Dubka (Lebanese)

Beat:	1	2	3	4	5	6
Foot:	L	R	L	L	L	R
Movement:	Forward	Back	Forward	Back	Hop as R crosses in front of L ankle	Step to R

8-beat Dubka: The eight-beat Dubka is also very common and the music is found on many recordings of Middle Eastern folk dance music.[4] See catalog (sent upon request) of Rashid Record Company, Atlantic Ave., Brooklyn, New York.

Beat:	1	2	3	4	5	6	7	8
Foot:	L	R	L	R	L	L	L	R
Movement:	Forward	Back	Forward	Back	forward	Back	Hop as R crosses in front of L ankle	Step to R

4. Several selections on this recording are also suitable acompaniment for the Hora.

SELECTED REFERENCES

1. BURNETT, MILLIE. *Melody, Movement and Language.* San Francisco: R. & E. Research Associates, 1973.
2. DOLL, EDNA and MARY JARMAN NELSON. *Rhythms Today.* Morristown, N. J.: Silver Burdett Co., 1965.
3. GRAY, VERA and RACHEL PERCIVAL. *Music, Movement and Mime for Children.* London: Oxford University Press, 1962.
4. HOOD, MARGUERITE. *Teaching Rhythm and Using Classroom Instruments.* Englewood Cliffs, N. J.: Prentice-Hall, 1970.
5. MYNATT, CONSTANCE V. and BERNARD D. KAIMAN. *Folk Dancing.* Dubuque, Iowa: Wm. C. Brown Co., 1967.
6. NASH, GRACE. *Verses and Movement.* Chicago: Kitchuig (Educational Division of Ludwig Press), 1967.
7. STECHER, MIRIAM et al. *Music and Movement Improvisation.* New York: The Macmillan Co., 1972.

14.

playing a small wind instrument

Whenever music is used with community groups, in camping, or any other recreational setting, the playing of small wind instruments can be helpful. Such experiences are initially inexpensive, moderately easy to learn, and fun! The use of a recorder-type wind instrument is the answer. Start the group on inexpensive plastic instruments before larger investments are made in the more refined and elaborate wooden recorders. Once the groups have had success playing together with these plastic instruments, there are generally a number of persons who would like to move on to more serious instruction with actual recorders. There are three plastic models available at most music stores; they are called by the trade names of "Flutophone," "Tonette," and "Songflute." If an order is for a fairly large number, special prices are frequently given. Instructions are usually included with the purchase of each instrument, nevertheless, the recreation director should be aware of the materials available and have a general working knowledge of how these instruments are played. Special assistance is available from within the music community, especially music teachers in the local schools.

GETTING STARTED

For our purposes here, instruction will be focused on the plastic instruments which are all played in the same manner. Because with most groups mastering the essentials of playing these instruments does not take too long, the recreation director should schedule instructional periods at convenient times when all can meet. A period of six weeks with a meeting for 1½ hours of instruction and rehearsal each week is a reasonable estimate. It is best to start new groups often, rather than to tire one group into the ground with too many and too frequent rehearsals—remember, this is a recreational activity! An intermediate or advanced group can always be arranged for those who desire it. This kind of planning must be left to the discretion of the director and will be governed by the nature of each recreational setting.

The first step in getting new groups started is to have them learn to hold and blow the instrument properly. When inspecting the instrument you will discover it has a row of holes on the top side and a single hole on the under side. The left hand thumb is used to cover the hole on the under side. Using the left hand, cover the first three holes from the top down with the first (pointer), second and third fingers. The little finger is not used.

Next, with the right hand, feel the underside of the instrument and discover a protruding nob. This is a thumb rest for the right hand. The first (pointer), second, third and fourth fingers are used to cover the remaining four holes.

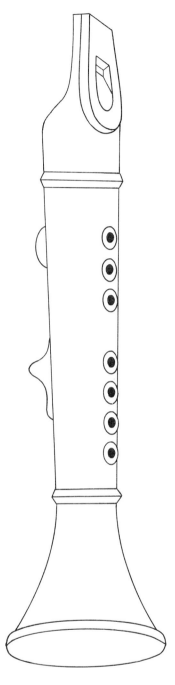

Figure 14.1

Make certain all holes are completely covered. Any escaping air will alter the pitch.

As soon as the correct way to hold the instrument is understood, the beginning player is ready to blow into it. Caution should be taken to prohibit any air to escape at the corners of the mouth. DO NOT BLOW HARD!! Forced blowing causes overtones and squawks to come through. Blow gently as one would blow a speck of dust from a mirror. Start each sound just as if the tongue were saying "too." Later, when it will be necessary to sustain the air flow for several pitches, just change the fingering to achieve a more smooth and connected melodic line (legato).

With the instrument held properly, the beginner is ready to play. On the underside of the instrument the thumb hole is covered with the left hand thumb and the top hole with the first finger (pointer) of the left hand. This is note B.

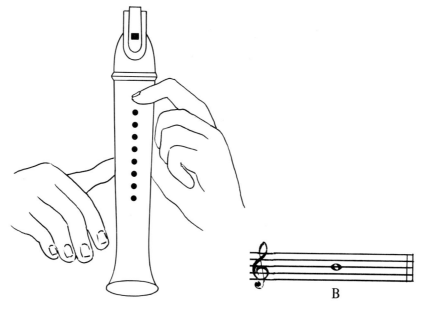

Figure 14.2

Balance the instrument with the right hand thumb on the thumb rest. Try blowing note B until it is a clear, sustained tone. Next, with the first finger of the left hand and the thumb still in place, cover the second hole with the second finger of the left hand (Figure 14.3). This is note A

Continue covering these holes and add the third finger of the left hand over the 3rd hole and blow note G (Figure 14.4)

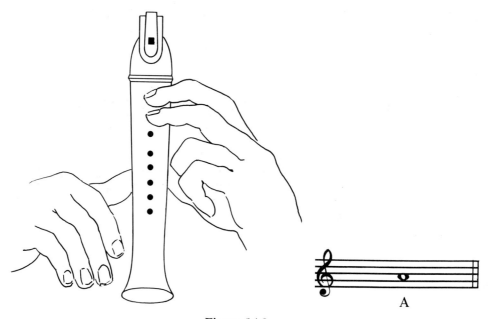

Figure 14.3

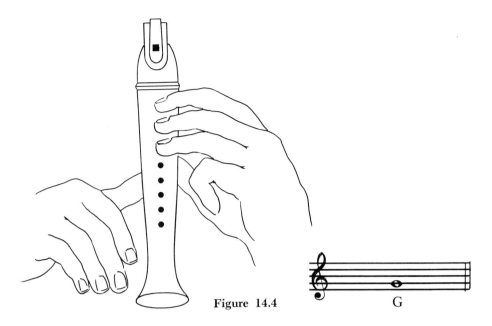

Figure 14.4

The player is now ready to play some simple melodies with these three notes: B, A and G.

Hot Cross Buns

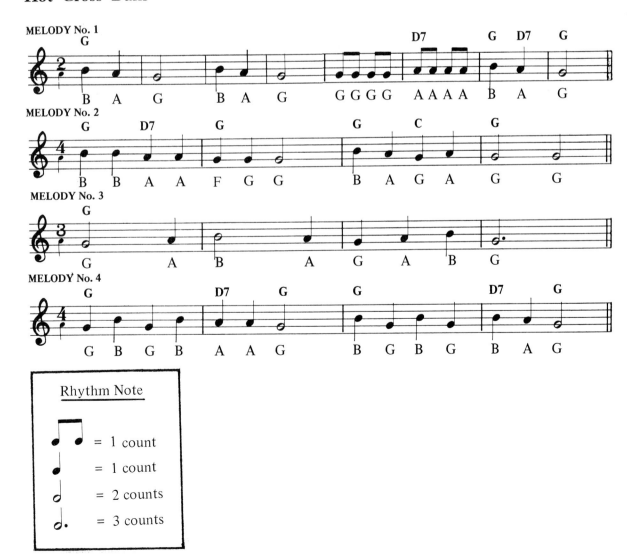

Now, start with the right hand. Cover the next hole after G with the first finger (pointer) of the right hand. Remember to keep the left hand holes tightly covered. This new fingering creates the note F (Figure 14.5).

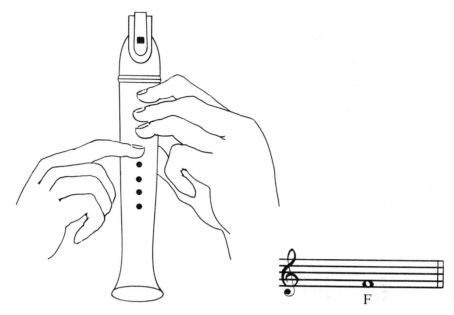

Figure 14.5

Try playing these melodies adding the new note F to the ones already learned.

MELODY No. 5

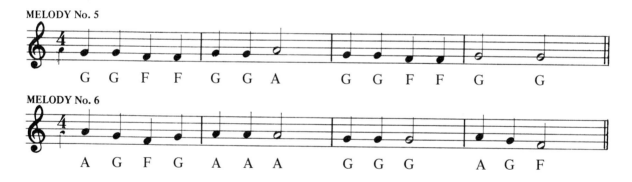

G G F F G G A   G G F F G   G

MELODY No. 6

A G F G A A A   G G G   A G F

With all the fingers used so far covering their respective holes, the next hole is covered with the second finger of the right hand to create the note E (Figure 14.6) and so on, covering each hole with each remaining finger of the right hand for notes D and C (Figures 14.7 and 14.8).

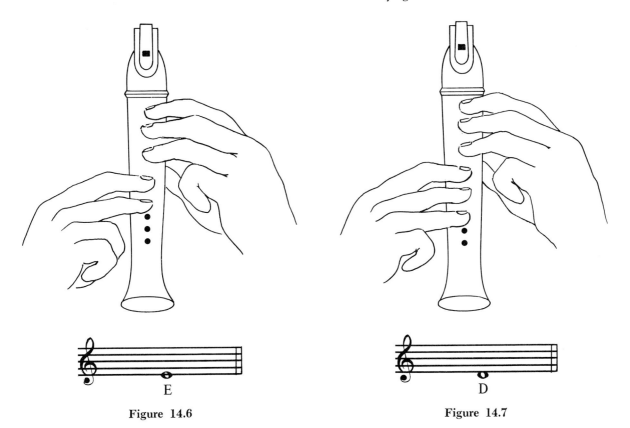

Figure 14.6

Figure 14.7

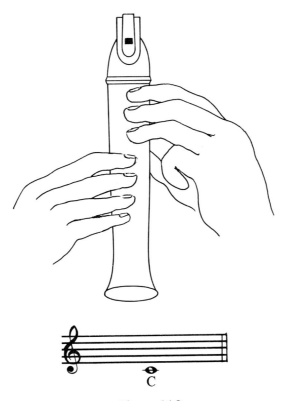

Figure 14.8

Care must be taken in playing these lower notes in order to not overblow. It will take some practice to release just the correct amount of breath at a certain pressure to achieve an even, controlled music tone.

The following melodies contain all the notes learned thus far. They have been labeled with their letter names to assist the player. It is necessary to associate the note on the staff with its proper letter name as soon as possible. This will make future music reading much easier.

March

Waltz

Skipping Fingers

To play note C, an octave (8 notes) above the last note learned, use only the thumb of the left hand to cover the one hole on the underside of the instrument (Figure 14.9). The note above this is D and is played by removing all the fingers of both hands and the left thumb, thus, uncovering all the holes (Figure 14.10).

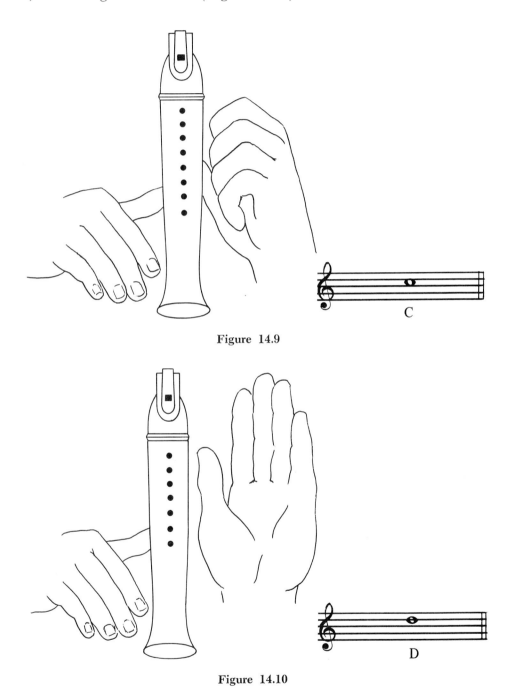

Figure 14.9

Figure 14.10

These melodies will assist the player to become familiar with the new notes: C and D.

MELODY No. 10

C   C   D   D   C   B   C   B   B   C   D   D   B   C

MELODY No. 11

D   C   B   D   C   B   C   D   C

Two more notes which will add to the enjoyment of playing this instrument are F Sharp (F♯) and B Flat (B♭). Many songs use these notes for singing in a comfortable vocal range, and they are needed when playing in the keys of G Major and F Major. To change the sound of F to F Sharp (F♯), the F must be raised ½ step. To play this, use the thumb, first, second and third fingers of the left hand and the second finger of the right hand (Figure 14.11).

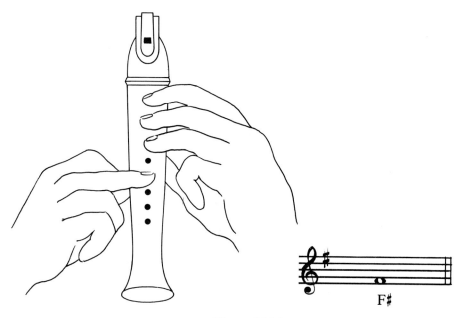

F♯

Figure 14.11

Practice these melodies to become acqainted with using an F Sharp (F♯).

MELODY No. 12

This tells the player to make every F an F♯

G   G   F♯ F♯ G   A   B   A   A   G   F♯ F♯ A   G

MELODY No. 13

D   C   B   A   G   F♯ G   A   G   F♯ F   G   A   G

To change the sound of B to B Flat (B♭), the B must be lowered a 1/2 step. To play B Flat (B♭), use the thumb and first finger of the left hand and the first finger of the right hand (Figure 14.12).

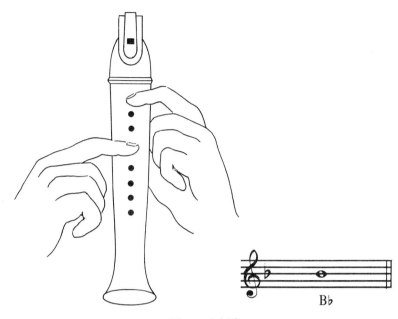

Figure 14.12

Practice these melodies to become acquainted with using a B Flat (B♭).

Selections like the following 5 part canon attributed to Praetorius generate interest and enjoyment in all recreational situations. Divide the group into 5 parts. Those playing in Part 1 begin, those in Part 2 start playing at the beginning when Part 1 reaches measure 3, as indicated in the music, and so on until all 5 parts are playing. Each part plays the selection five times.

Five Part Canon

SELECTED REFERENCES

1. BRIMHALL, JOHN. *Tooter No. 1.* New York: Charles Hansen, 1966.
2. DUSCHENES, MARIO. *Method for the Recorder.* New York: Associated Music Publishers, Inc., 1957.
3. JOHN, ROBERT W. and CHARLES H. DOUGLAS. *Playing Social and Recreational Instruments.*
4. MARSH, MARY VAL, et al. *Spectrum of Music,* "Playing the Recorder." New York: The Macmillan Company, 1975.

15.

finding, making and using
your own instruments

For a rewarding recreational experience, nothing is more satisfying for any group, young or old, than to create or discover various types of instruments and play them. Exploring the many possibilities inherent in discarded materials is, in itself, an exciting activity.

The simplest instruments to make are percussive or rhythmic. They can be produced with a little imagination and add a personal enrichment to all singing and moving activities. For the more industrious persons, homemade instruments which produce various pitches can augment the pleasure and creativeness of almost all musical experiences in recreation.

The following are ideas to guide the recreational leader in getting started with this interesting activity.

PERCUSSION INSTRUMENTS

Drums. These essential instruments can be made from both small and large cans with membrane or rubber stretched across the open head. Large cardboard or plastic containers inverted so the bottoms can be struck also make good drums. If nothing else is available, turn the waste basket over and "play" on its under side. This can serve as a drumlike sound source.

Gongs. This sound can be simulated by hanging large ash can covers by their handles and striking them with a padded mallet of some sort.

Maracas. These can be made by partially filling various sizes of plastic pill boxes with pebbles, rice or sand. The same sound effect can be obtained by using metal beer and soft drink cans. Be sure to cover the opening with masking tape after you add the beans or pebbles. If one lives in a locality where gourds are grown, these offer a variety of shapes and sizes. When dried and filled with beans, rice, sand, or even some dried lintels they produce various sounds when shaken. Any of these devices produce an authentic maraca sound.

Tambourines. These are constructed from a 10″ round or square piece of plywood with pop bottle caps loosely nailed around the edges.

Wood Blocks. These are of all the easiest to make. Select various sizes of wood from a lumber company's scrap box and arrange them to produce certain qualities of sound as the wooden pieces are struck with a mallet.

Sand Blocks. These are made from 4″ pieces of wood sawed from a 2 x 4 with sandpaper tacked across on one side. Make two of them and scrape them against each other for special sound effects.

Guiros. The sound of this interesting Latin-American instrument can be imitated by scraping the scrubbing surface of an old-fashioned washboard with a small wooden dowel about the size of a pencil.

Rasp or Scraper. This instrument has its roots in several American Indian tribes. Obtain an old broom handle or a 4 foot length of wooden dowel. With a sharp penknife, cut regularly spaced deep notches for about two feet in the middle of the wooden shaft. Hold the rasp with one hand while the other hand scrapes a pencil across the notches. The end of the rasp farthest away from the player should rest on a drum, a basket, an inverted flower pot, or a large tin can, in order to amplify the sound created by the scraping. Many different effets and unique sounds can be discovered that will fascinate both player and listener.

PITCHED INSTRUMENTS

Wash Tub Bass. The sound of a string bass can be produced from a contraption that is fairly easy to assemble. All that is needed is a large galvanized wash tub, a wooden pole about 4 feet long (a discarded broom handle will do nicely), a piece of very strong twine or even an actual string bass string purchased at your local music store, plus a bolt, a nut, and two washers.

Prepare the wooden pole by grooving one end and notching the other (Figure 15.1). The groove is for tying one end of the twine; the notch is to anchor the pole to the rim on the bottom of the tub.

The tub is prepared by drilling or punching a hole of the size to accommodate the bolt used in the center of the bottom. Assemble the nut, bolt, and washers as indicated in Figure 15.2, and tie one end of the twine or regular bass string to the bolt before it is tightened.

The bolt and twine will be outside the inverted tub.
Next, with the tub inverted, locate the rim and put the notched end of the wooden pole on it. Measure the distance from the grooved end of the pole to the bolt and tie off the twine. This should be taut. Now, the instrument is ready to experiment with in producing various pitches. With one foot on the inverted tub, the player grasps the twine and end of pole with one hand while the other hand is used to pluck the twine.

The pitch can be varied, changing the pressure by bending gently the pole away from the tub (Figure 15.4). The more taut the twine, the higher the pitch; lessen the pressure and the pitch will drop. Be very careful not to put too much pressure on the pole as it will snap the twine. A little practice will produce the desired results.

Mouth Bow. This interesting instrument is sometimes called an Apache violin. String both notched ends of a curved stick as you would for a regular hunting bow. Bite into one end and place the other end on something to serve as an amplifier of sound. This could be a box, tin can, plastic bowl, or a dried gourd. Balance the bow with mouth and one hand while the other hand plucks the string. Pitches can be adjusted by changing shape of mouth and the pressures applied to the curved stick.

Musical Ruler. Try holding a wooden ruler against a table or desk with one hand and snap its protruding edge with the other hand. In this way, various pitches can be produced by changing the length of the overhang of the ruler. Once a desired pitch is found, the ruler can be marked. A two or three pitch pattern (ostinato) can easily be mastered; this will add to the accompaniment of songs.

Glass Bottles. Different pitches can be created by putting water into various sizes of glass bottles and blowing across their openings as one would blow a traditional flute.

Figure 15.1

Figure 15.2

Figure 15.3

Fig. 15.4

Hose. Another idea for making a pitch instrument is to cut a discarded garden hose in various lengths starting with a 5 inch piece. Then, blow across the opening of each in the same manner used with the bottles. Be sure the other end of each piece of hose is sealed with either putty or masking tape. After a few attempts at cutting the hose and testing pitches, a pentatonic scale (Do, Re, Mi, Sol, La) can be created. Mount each piece of hose on a strip of 2 inch board with a strong glue to resemble the "Pipes of Pan."

Sounds from the Scrap Basket. Another source for a homemade pitch instrument is the scrap basket in a welder's shop. Various lengths of metal bars can be chosen for their quality and pitches; then mounted loosely on parallel strips of rubber or plastic tubing. These metal bars are played like a xylophone with a mallet. The same xylophone effect can be obtained from using various lengths of hard wood gleaned from a scrap basket at the local lumber company.

Brake Drum. For a heavy metallic sound, especially good with Calypso music, an automobile brake drum is ideal. These can be easily found in automobile grave yards or from junk dealers. When struck with a metal object they "speak" in sharp, commanding sounds.

Water Glasses. Bell sounds can be created by striking various sizes of water glasses with a spoon. The pitches are changed by the amount of water added to each glass. Suspended clay flower pots, arranged according to size, will produce interesting darker bell tones when struck with a wooden mallet. Large nails and other bits of metal hung in the same manner can produce bell-like sounds when struck with other metallic objects.

The following song is an example of how these homemade instruments may be used to increase the pleasure of and involvement in this kind of activity. The song is written in a pentatonic scale (F G A C D). Sing it first in unison until everyone is familiar with the tune and rhythm. Then divide the group into two sections and sing the song as indicated in round form. Group Two starts at the beginning as Group One begins measure two. Finally, add some of the homemade instruments. The following steps are suggested only as starters. It is always a good idea to ask for suggestions from the group, especially in recreational settings.

Sing and Play

J. M. BATCHELLER

Step #1. Using quart glass soda bottles, tune them by adjusting the water level to the pitches F and C. Invite two persons from the group to play them together, thus creating an harmonic interval of a 5th, frequently called a *Bourdon*. These two players will play on the 2nd and 4th beats of every measure throughout the song.

Glass Bottles

Beats 1 2 3 4

Step #2. Next, have a person play the double bass (the galvanized tub) on just 2 pitches: F and C. This player will perform F on the 1st beat and C on the 3rd beat throughout the song.

Double Bass

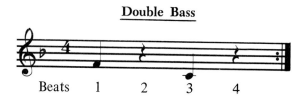

Beats 1 2 3 4

Step #3. Ask another person in the group to play the largest and lowest sounding drum in your collection of homemade instruments on the 1st beat of every measure.

Drum

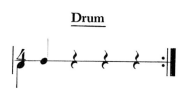

Step #4. Give another person a set of homemade maracas and still another a woodblock. They will play the following rhythm throughout the song.

Maracas

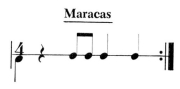

SELECTED REFERENCES

1. HOFSINDE, ROBERT. *Indian Music Makers.* New York: William Morrow and Company, 1967.
2. JOHNSTON, THOMAS F. "How to Make a Tsonga Zylophone," *Music Educators Journal,* 63, 3 (November, 1976), p. 38.
3. KETTLEKAMP, LARRY. *Flutes, Whistles and Reeds.* New York: William Mirrow, 1962.
4. MANDELL, MURIEL and ROBERT E. WOOD. *Make Your Own Musical Instruments.* New York: Sterling, 1959.
5. MORALES, HUMBERT. *Latin American Rhythm Instruments.* New York: H. Adler Publishers Corp., 1954.
6. SEEGER, PETER. "The Steel Drum: A New Folk Instrument," *Journal of American Folklore,* 71 (January-March), p. 52.
7. WEIDEMANN, CHARLES C. *Music in Sticks and Stones,* How to Construct and Play Simple Instruments. New York: Exposition Press, 1967.
8. WEIL, LISE. *Things That Go Bang.* New York: McGraw-Hill Book Company, 1969.

16.

music and olympics: another dimension

And what shall be the education of our heroes? Can we
find a better than the traditional sort?—and this has two
divisions, gymnastics for the body and music for the soul.

Plato
The Republic

There are many ways in which the themes of the Olympic games can be infused into a recreation program. Both sports and music support an individual's search for expression. They involve the values of commitment and discipline in striving toward a goal. They are overt demonstrations of man's ability to participate actively in worthwhile endeavors; and, in an educational setting, they can play a role in helping students to develop self-confidence and awareness of others.

As a part of the music program, experiences can be adapted to bring out, through involvement with singing, listening, and playing instruments, the concepts of the Olympics within the established goals of musical sensitivity. For example, in and of itself part-singing is an experience in responsibility and cooperation. Each singer becomes responsible for the end product. The same is true of ensemble playing, where interdependence within the group will make the final performance. Listening perceptively to music requires discipline and concentration. Often the text or the descriptive nature of a piece of music can be related to themes of brotherhood, patriotism, and nationalism. Also, musical selections representative of national styles and folk idioms can add to cultural awareness.

Another important aspect of music study is that it provides an ennobling way to spend our leisure time—the way the Greeks perceived leisure. Our present society sometimes views leisure pursuits as being largely passive and "resting" in nature. We would be better off as a people if we practiced the Greek ideal of active participation in a worthwhile experience as the best form of leisure and recreation. Music is one of these experiences.

This chapter is based on materials by SM as found in *The Olympics: An Educational Opportunity, Enrichment Units*, to be copyrighted by the United States Olympic Committee, 1981. These materials are used with the permission of the United States Olympic Committee.

In other words, a broad view of the Olympics can involve placing more emphasis on participation and the challenge of struggling to reach a goal rather than an athletic prowess for its own sake.

Walter Umminger, in his book *Supermen, Heroes, and Gods,* writes:

"The Greeks do not appear to have been interested in measuring and recording individual feats—in 'records,' in other words. . . . Competing, that was what counted, and if possible putting up a better performance than the other competitors. There were, as time went on, so many classes to compete in. If you were not going to measure yourself against the sprinters or the boxers, you could try improvising poetry, or dancing, or speech making, or playing music—there was even an Olympic prize for trumpet sounding. The trumpeters might be challenged for the same prize by heralds, who would compete against them in the Echo Porch, a long arcade facing west across the center of the Altis. The strength and clarity with which messages could be sent, whether by bugle or by town crier, were essential for public communication, so the contest of both for the same prize was quite appropriate. We are so used to 'athletics' meaning only physical exercises and sports that we have to remind ourselves of what the word meant to the ancient Greeks. An 'athlete' was quite simply a 'competitor' from the word for prize: athlon."

OBJECTIVES

Among the objectives of activities linking music with concepts of the Olympics are the following:

—Through active participation in ensemble singing and playing of instruments, students can experience personal and social interaction with others.

—By using gross and fine motor movements when learning to play musical instruments or move to the rhythm of music, students may recognize the value of continuous practice in developing a skill.

—By creating and notating their own musical compositions, students may gain the power to express inner qualities of feeling and learn the value of attention to the refinement and ultimate improvement of their work.

—By playing and singing in music festivals, and other public performances, students may experience group solidarity, teamwork, and develop the self-confidence which comes from working toward a recognized goal.

—By learning to sing, play, and listen to the music of various national groups, students may become more sensitive to the feelings of nationalism as reflections of cultural roots.

—By singing, playing, and listening to music from other nations, students may become culturally aware of their common brotherhood with the people of the world.

ACTIVITIES AND EXPERIENCES

The following suggestions will involve participants in a variety of activities relating the Olympic spirit and music. While most are appropriate for group settings, several can be adapted for use by individuals or pairs.

Songs of Brotherhood
"How Good It Is My Brothers"

ROUND-ISRAEL

How good it is my bro - thers to meet _ and sing to - geth - er.

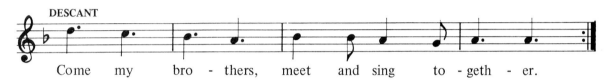

Oh how good it is to meet _ and sing to - geth - er.

DESCANT

Come my bro - thers, meet and sing to - geth - er.

Musical Experiences: Sing the above song with enthusiasm and rhythmic flow. Sing as a round. Add the descant, which can be sung an octave lower for chanting voices. Create an ostinato by using a melodic or rhythmic fragment taken from a song and repeat throughout. Add the instrument in improvised or pre-determined fashion. Accompany with harmonic instruments (autoharp, etc.). Refine both singing and playing by describing ways they could be improved, given the expressive and musical qualities of the song.

Concepts of Olympism: Discuss the role which songs can play in developing feelings of unity and brotherhood among a given group. Allow group to suggest other songs taken from their past experience that provide the same impetus, such as "He's Got the Whole World in His Hands."

UNIVERSAL MUSICAL SPIRIT

Musical Experiences: Chant the "Hello's" below. Discover the differences between duple and triple meter. Change the chants by inserting different "Hello's" from other countries. Notate new patterns if desired. Add expressive controls by varying dynamic levels and accents. Add instruments.

DUPLE

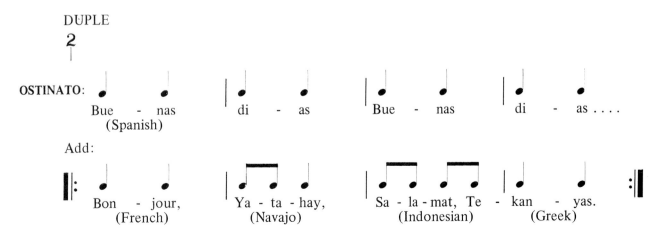

OSTINATO: Bue - nas di - as Bue - nas di - as . . . .
(Spanish)

Add: Bon - jour, Ya - ta - hay, Sa - la - mat, Te - kan - yas.
(French) (Navajo) (Indonesian) (Greek)

TRIPLE

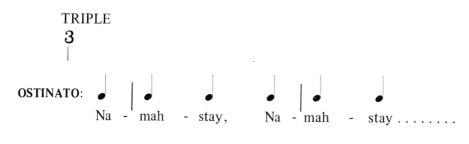

OSTINATO:

Na - mah - stay,   Na - mah - stay . . . .

Add:

O - hi - o   go - zai - mas,   Eh - he - len   wa   se - he - len.

Other Languages: "Jen Dobre"—Polish; "Guten Tag"—German;
"Neehowma"—Mandarin; "Aloha"—Hawaiian;
"Jambo Sana"—Swahili.

Concepts of Olympism: Have group describe their own cultural background, countries from which ancestors came, languages spoken at home, etc. Compile a list of greetings taken from the class, and create additional chants. Discuss the feelings of acceptance that come from sharing some aspect of our culture with others.

Songs from many countries are available from: World Around Songs, Rt. 5, Box 398, Burnsville, North Carolina 28714.

SPORTS IN RHYTHM

Musical Experiences: Establish the tempo and chant the "sports" below. They range in difficulty from primary through intermediate. Some ideas for presentation:

1. Discuss which sports are appropriate for summer and which for winter games.
2. Chant first in unison. Divide group and chant both parts together. Try in round form.
3. Begin with ostinato. Add instruments appropriate to the idea of the sport, if possible.
4. Create new chants or add more to those already given.
5. Read from notation. Alter words to change notation and continue reading new patterns according to level of students in music reading experiences.
6. List several of the sports of the Olympic games. Describe some of the achievements and skills inherent in these, such as, accuracy, interdependence, etc. Discuss the ways in which musical performances require the same qualities.
7. Try playing the "Fencing Round" with instruments and no words. Discover the need for concentration at the time of entrance of each part. Create another chant using the actions of a different sport. Discuss the complexities of sports when played well. Compare with musical performance.

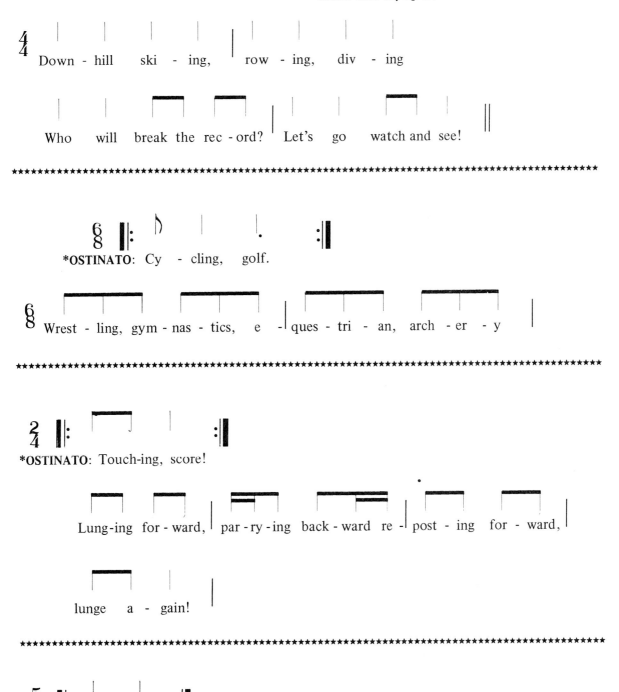

4/4 Down - hill ski - ing, row - ing, div - ing
Who will break the rec - ord? Let's go watch and see!

6/8 *OSTINATO: Cy - cling, golf.

6/8 Wrest - ling, gym - nas - tics, e - ques - tri - an, arch - er - y

2/4 *OSTINATO: Touch-ing, score!

Lung-ing for - ward, par - ry - ing back - ward re - post - ing for - ward,

lunge a - gain!

5/4 *OSTINATO: Box - ing

Ice skat - ing, rug - by, ten - nis and div - ing

*Chant Throughout

Note: In the following chant, notice the *shift of accent* when chanting them together. Try them first as individual chants.

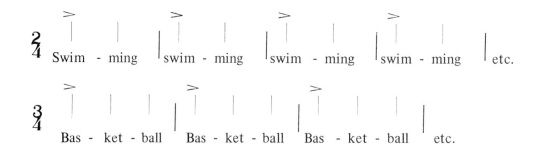

Concepts of Olympism: List several of the sports of the Olympic games. Describe some of the achievements and skills inherent in these, such as accuracy, interdependency, etc. Discuss the ways in which musical performances require the same qualities.

THE CHALLENGE OF NEW FRONTIERS

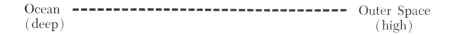

Ocean — Outer Space
(deep)   (high)

Two composers, Alan Hovhaness and Gyorgy Ligeti, have written compositions that are on the frontiers of both musical and technological progress. They are real "musical" pioneers. Both can be found in *Sound, Shape and Symbol,* New Dimensions Series, American Book Company.

Musical Experiences: Listen to "And God Created Great Whales," by Hovhaness. Follow a listening guide or call chart. The composer has used tape recordings of humpback whales singing underwater as the basis for this work. The tapes were recorded off the shore of Bermuda by a research zoologist. They have been "shaped" by using higher and lower speeds and integrated into an orchestral work. Discuss the rondo form of the music when the whale songs are alternated with a pentatonic theme by the orchestra. Listen to "Atmospheres" by Ligeti. Discover the musical ways this composer used electronics to give the illusion of outer space, with vast distances and the feeling of the unknown.

Concepts of the Olympics: Discuss the many ways man has reflected human development and advancement. Relate to the idea of responsible leadership in every field—including music. Use the composers above as examples of muscians who were interested in going beyond the usual in their field and have, thereby, contributed to progress.

MUSIC AND NATIONALISM

Preliminary Experiences. Begin by discussing the meaning of nationalism with the group, na-tion-al-ism, n: loyalty and devotion to a nation. . . . Recite the pledge of allegiance with the students. Write the words to the pledge on the chalkboard.

—What do these words mean to you?

—Why do we recite this pledge in school?

—When do we sing the national anthem? Why do we sing it?

—What are our other "best known" patriotic songs?

—What are some other ways in which we display our loyalty to our nation?

—What do we mean when we say that the flag ("Stars and Stripes") is a symbol of our nation?

—What are other United States national symbols? (Bald Eagle; Uncle Sam)

1. After discussing the meaning of the stars and stripes on our flag, ask the group to make a small, 8½" x 11" replica of our flag using colored paper, crayons, felt pens, etc.
2. Show the group pictures of earlier United States flags and discuss the reasons for the different designs and symbols.
3. Sing patriotic songs of the group's choice. Follow by listening to "Stars and Stripes" by John Philip Sousa. What in the music makes it such a rousing, stirring "crowd pleaser?"

    Concepts of the Olympics: Discuss the feelings of pride in achievement when one is representing something outside of oneself, such as school, city, country, etc. What responsibilities go along with being a member of a group?

SOUNDS OF SPORTS

The following are brief activity suggestions for use in any group recreational situation.

ACTIVITY 1 . . . Using the newspaper, have each person make a sport and sound dictionary. Find as many words in the newspaper from A-Z, which either represent sounds made by or during an Olympic activity or are the names of sports events. Make and illustrate a dictionary using these words. If appropriate, have the group compose brief defintions as well. For example:

> A: applause; archery
> B: bang; basketball; boxing
> C: canoeing; cheer

ACTIVITY 2 . . . Collect pictures of musical instruments, or bring real instruments to class. Classify the instruments as *string, percussion,* or *wind.* Decide which part of the instrument must vibrate to make the sound.

ACTIVITY 3 . . . Make a band with "found materials" such as bottles, combs, pots, pans, wood, nails, and rubber bands. Compose an Olympics-inspired musical arrangement for these "instruments." Perform it as a group.

ACTIVITY 4 . . . Play a variety of musical selections which suggest typical sounds and sports of the Olympics. Have the group identify various Olympic activities or sports that would seem to match the music. Discuss.

ACTIVITY 5 . . . Ask each person to choose one Olympic sport to pantomime. Choose a musical selection to accompany the pantomime that would describe the mood of the sport. The music might be relaxing, boisterous, bubbly, sweet, or uplifting. Let each person act out the pantomime and have the others guess what Olympic sport or activity it is. Decide whether or not the music helped establish a mood.

ACTIVITY 6 . . . Play a game of listening with your group. Ask them to close their eyes. Ask for a volunteer to begin the game by making a sound that would represent an activity or sport. The person who guesses the sound correctly becomes the next one to make a sound for the others to identify.

PROGRAM IDEAS

The "Grand" event is an integral part of games and competition. Music can become an essential part of an "Olympiad," or can be an example of an Olympic-like event—in and of itself. The following program ideas can be used separately or combined with other events for a broader, larger performance.

1. For an Olympic Festival that takes place in a gym or auditorium which can be darkened, have a chorus march in at the beginning singing "This Little Light of Mine" (Spiritual), holding flashlights reminiscent of the torch at the beginning of the actual Olympic games.

2. As a part of an Olympic program, have participants prepare a movement sequence to go with the words of "It's a Small World," while another group acts as a chorus to sing the song.

3. Have a flag-waving ceremony with the Olympic flag and the U.S. flag, as well as several flags from various countries. Flags in front could be waving in a 4/4 conducting pattern as a background chorus (or audience) sings "There Are Many Flags in Many Lands."

4. For younger children, present a medley of songs on one sport topic, dramatize or act out one, and/or add accompanying bell and rhythm patterns with instruments. An example might be "Row, Row Your Boat," "My Paddle's Keen and Bright," and "Michael Row Your Boat Ashore."

5. Try an Olympic Anthem Competition. This could be a combined project for both the instrumentalists and vocalists. Discuss possible ideas for lyrics, e.g., brotherhood, nationalism, freedom, etc. Select judges, including a local professional or semi-professional musician, if possible. Perform the winner at an "Olympic Game" or school assembly. Include the preparation of the judging form, thus giving participants experience in evaluation and criticism. A guide for such a form might be: overall appeal, range, consequence of text with music.

6. Older Groups can sing excerpts from *Lest We Forget*, an American Cantata sung at the Summer 1932 Olympic Games in Los Angeles. Bring out the style in the writing for this musical period. (Music available from the Library of Congress, Attention: Mrs. Charles Sens, Music Reference Department, Library of Congress, Washington, D. C. 20540.)

7. Instrumental Groups can perform the following (or similar) fanfares. Discuss the importance of "entrance" and "exit" music at festivals, games, and other events throughout history. The list below represents fanfares of different styles and periods. End this study by inviting gifted persons to compose their own fanfare to be performed at the local "Olympics" or other similar event. (All of the pieces below can be ordered from Robert King Music Company, 112 Main Street, North Easton, Massachusetts 02356.)

   > "Olympic Fanfare" from *Bugler's Dream*, Leo Arnaud
   >   (as heard on ABC Olympic telecasts)
   > "Fanfare" C.P.E. Bach (3 trumpets, timpani).
   > "Concerto" Altenburg (7 trumpets, timpani).
   > "Fanfare" William Walton (Full Brass Choir).
   > "Fanfare for the Common Man" Aaron Copland (Full
   >   Brass, Percussion).

8. Perform an appropriate arrangement, (Full Orchestration, Brass Ensemble, etc.,) of "Rondo" by Mouret, sometimes known as "The Masterpiece." Relate it to the theme of the Masterpiece Theater on TV. Also point out that this selection was used for the 1976 Olympic Games in Canada, (available from King Company, see above).

SELECTED REFERENCES

CHESTER, DAVID. *The Olympic Games Handbook*: *An Authentic History of Both the Ancient and Modern Olympic Games, Complete Results and Records.* New York: Scribner, 1975.

COOTE, JAMES. *A Picture History of the Olympics.* New York: Macmillan, 1972.

DEVANEY, JOHN. *Great Olympic Champions.* New York: Putnam, 1967.

DIEM, CARL. *The Olympic Idea.* Stuttgart, Germany: Verlag Karl Hofmann (7060 Schorndorf bei Stuttgart), 1970.

DURANT, JOHN. *Highlights of the Olympics*: *From Ancient Times to the Present.* New York: Hastings House, 1977.

GAULT, FRANK and CLARE. *Stories from the Olympics*: *From 776 B.C. to Now.* New York: Walker and Company, 1976.

GELMAN, STEVE. *Young Olympic Champions.* New York: Grosset and Dunlap, 1973.

KIERAN, JOHN and ARTHUR DALEY and PAT JORDAN. *The Story of the Olympic Games*, 776 B.C. to 1976. Rev. ed. Philadelphia: Lippincott, 1977.

McWHIRTER, NORRIS and ROSS, eds. *Guiness Book of Olympic Records*: *Complete Roll of Olympic Medal Winners.* New York: Bantam, 1976.

U.S. Olympic Committee. *The Olympiads*: *An Educational Opportunity.* Olympic House, Colorado Springs, Colorado, 1981.

U.S. Olympic Committee. *The Olympic Games.* Olympic House, Colorado Springs, Colorado.

YALOURIS, NIKOLAS, ed. *The Olympic Games Through the Ages.* New Rochelle, N.Y.: Caratzas Bros., 1977.

III.

musical examples for recreational singing and playing

The Star-Spangled Banner
(Standard Service Version)

MUSIC BY JOHN STAFFORD SMITH
WORDS BY FRANCIS SCOTT KEY

America

SAMUEL FRANCIS SMITH

ATTRIBUTED TO
HENRY CAREY

America the Beautiful

KATHARINE LEE BATES

SAMUEL A. WARD

1. O beau-ti-ful for spa-cious skies, For am-ber waves of grain, For pur-ple moun tain maj-es-ties A-bove the fruit-ed plain! A-mer-i-ca! A-mer-i-ca! God shed His grace on thee, And crown thy good with broth-er-hood From sea to shin-ing sea!

2. O beautiful for Pilgrim feet,
   Whose stern impassioned stress
   A thoroughfare for freedom beat
   Across the wilderness.
   America! America! God mend thine every
       flaw,
   Confirm thy soul in self-control,
   Thy liberty in law.

3. O beautiful for heroes proved
   In liberating strife,
   Who more than self their country loved,
   And mercy more than life.
   America! America! May God thy gold refine
   Till all success be nobleness
   And every gain divine.

4. O beautiful for patriot dream
   That sees beyond the years,
   Thine alabaster cities gleam
   Undimmed by human tears.
   America! America! God shed His grace on thee,
   And crown thy good with brotherhood
   From sea to shining sea.

All Through the Night

BRITISH ISLES

1. Sleep, my child and peace at-tend thee, All through the night;

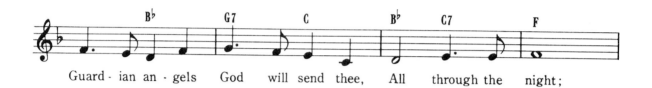

Guard-ian an-gels God will send thee, All through the night;

Soft the drow-sy hours are creep-ing, Hill and vale in slum-ber steep-ing;

I my lov-ing vig-il keep-ing, All through the night.

2. While the moon her watch is keeping
   All through the night;
   While the heavy world is sleeping
   All through the night;
   O'er thy spirit gently stealing,
   Visions of delight revealing,
   Breathes a pure and holy feeling
   All through the night.

1. Holl amrantaur sèr ddywedant, Ar hyd y nos,
   "Dyma'r ffordd i fro gogoniant," Ar hyd y nos.
   Golen arall yw tywyllwch, I arddaug os gwir brydferthweh,
   Teulu'r nef oedd mewn tawelwch, Ar hyd y nos.

Buffalo Gals

(THREE LITTLE GIRLS)

With Animation

COOL WHITE

1. As I was walk-ing down the street, down the street, down the street, A

pret - ty gal I chanced to meet, Oh she was fair to see.

Chorus

Oh, Buf-fa-lo Gals won't you come out to-night, come out to-night, come out to-night? Oh,

Buf-fa-lo Gals won't you come out to-night, and dance by the light of the moon?

2. I asked her if she'd stop and talk, stop and talk, stop and talk,
   Her feet took up the whole sidewalk, and left no room for me.
3. I asked her if she'd be my wife, be my wife, be my wife,
   Then I'd be happy all my life, if she'd marry me.

Blow the Man Down

Rapidly

CHANTEY

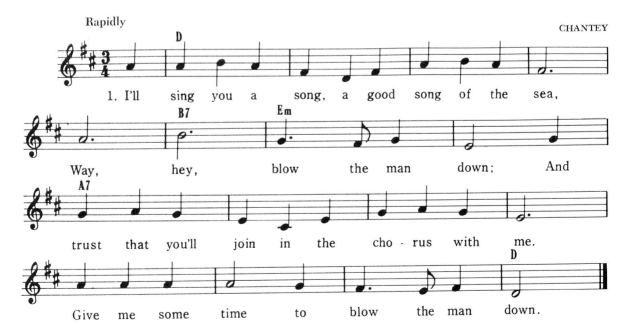

1. I'll sing you a song, a good song of the sea,

Way, hey, blow the man down; And

trust that you'll join in the cho - rus with me.

Give me some time to blow the man down.

Blow Ye Winds

'Tis ad-ver-tised in Bos-ton, New York, and Buf-fa-lo, Five hun-dred brave A-mer-i-cans, A-whal-ing for to go___, sing-ing

Chorus

Blow, ye winds, in the morn-ing, Blow, ye winds, heigh-ho, Haul a-way your run-ning gear, And blow, ye winds, heigh-ho.

Shoo, Fly, Don't Bother Me

BILLY REEVES   FRANK CAMPBELL

Shoo, fly, don't both-er me, Shoo, fly, don't both-er me, Shoo, fly, don't both-er me, For I be-long to some-bod-y.

Shoo, Fly, Don't Bother Me

1. I feel, I feel, I feel, I feel like a morn-ing star, I
feel, I feel, I feel, I feel like a morn-ing star.

2. I feel, I feel, I feel, I feel, like my mother said,
Like angels pouring 'lasses down on my little head.

Eency, Weency Spider

ACTION SONG

Een-cy, ween-cy spi-der went up the wa-ter spout;
Down came the rain and washed the spi-der out;
Out came the sun and dried up all the rain, And the
een-cy ween-cy spi-der went up the spout a-gain.

Yankee Doodle

U. S.

1. O fath'r and I went down to camp, a - long with Cap-tain Good' - in, And there we saw the men and boys as thick as hast - y pud - din'.

Chorus

Yan - kee Doo-dle keep it up, Yan - kee Doo-dle Dan - dy,

Mind the mu - sic and the step, And with the girls be hand - y.

La Raspe

TR. MAURICE TALBOT

MEXICO

With click-ing of cas - ta - nets and jin-gle of tam - bou - rine, All work of the day for - got, and danc-ing to - night is queen. We're danc - ing a dance from old Mex - i - co, La la la la la la; Our steps light and gay, and our hearts a - glow, La la la la la la.

Frog Went Courting

KENTUCKY

1. Frog went court-ing, he did ride, Rink-tum bod-dy mitch-a - cam - bo.

Sword and buck-ler by his side, Rink-tum bod-dy mitch-a - cam - bo.

Chorus

Kim - an - i - ro, down to Cai - ro, Kim - an - i - ro,

Cai - ro; Strad-a - lad-da - lad-a - bod-dy,

Lad-da-bod-dy-link-tum, Rink-tum bod-dy mitch-a - cam - bo.

2. To the lady mouse said he, "Will you kindly marry me?" etc.
3. Who can make the wedding gown? Old Miss Rat from London town, etc.
4. Then there came a big Tom Cat. So long frog and mouse and rat! etc.

Finlandia

SM AND JB

JEAN SIBELIUS

1. God grant us peace and depth of under stand-ing,____
____ That we may live and share the world as one. ____
____ With joy and love we seek all men as brothers, ____
____ And come to feel the free-dom just be - gun. ____
____ As brothers all we share this world to - geth er, ____
____ And light the can - dle of our ris ing sun. ____

2. Through storm and stress thy heroes shall not fail thee,
Though perils press them hard on every hand;
God grant them strength and courage when the need be,
Clear eyes to see, and hearts to understand.
God lead thee on through nobleness to triumph,
God make thee great, my own native land.

Every Time I Feel the Spirit

SPIRITUAL

Eve - ry time I ___ feel the spir - it ___ mov - ing
in my heart ___ I will pray. Eve - ry time I ___ feel the
spir - it ___ mov - ing in my heart ___ I will pray.

Verse

1. Up - on the moun - tain ___ when my Lord spoke, Out of His
mouth came ___ fire and smoke. Up - on the moun - tain ___ when my Lord
spoke, Out of His mouth came ___ fire and smoke.

2. Looked all around me, it sure looked fine;
   I asked my Lord if it were mine.
   Looked all around me, it sure looked fine;
   I asked my Lord if it were mine.

We Wish You a Merry Christmas

ENGLAND

1. We wish you a mer-ry Christ-mas, We wish you a mer-ry Christ-mas, We wish you a mer-ry Christ-mas, and a hap-py New Year.

Chorus

Good ti-dings to you and to all your kin, Good ti-dings for Christ-mas and all the New Year.

2. Please bring us some figgy pudding, please bring us some figgy pudding,
Please bring us some figgy pudding, please bring it right here.

3. We won't leave until we get some, we won't leave until we get some,
We won't leave until we get some, please bring it right here.

At the Gate of Heaven

(A LA PUERTO DEL CIELO)

DR. A. D. ZANZIG   SPAIN

1. At the gate of heav'n lit-tle shoes they are sell-ing

For the lit-tle bare-foot-ed an-gels there dwell-ing.

Chorus

Slum-ber, my ba-by, slum-ber my ba-by,

Slum-ber, my ba-by, a-rru, a-rru.

2. God will bless the children so peacefully sleeping,
   God will help the mothers whose love they are keeping.

1. A la puerto del cielo Venden zapatos,
   Para los angelitos que endan descalzos,
   Duermete, niño, duermete, niño,
   Duermete, niño, arru, arru.

2. A los niños que duermen Dios los bendice,
   A las madres que velan Dios las asiste,
   Duermete, niño, duermete, niño,
   Duermete, niño, arru, arru.

Every Night When the Sun Goes Down

1. Oh, ev - 'ry - night _____ when the sun goes down, _____

_____ Oh, ev - 'ry - night _____ when the sun goes down, _____

_____ Oh, ev - 'ry night _____ when the sun goes down, _____

_____ I hang down my head _____ and mourn-ful cry. _____

2. True love, don't weep, true love don't mourn, (three times)
I'm going away from this old town.

3. Oh, how I wish that train would come, (three times)
To take me back to where I'm from.

4. And when that train does finally come, (three times)
I'm going back to my old home.

5. Oh, how I wish my babe was born,
And sitting on his daddy's knee,
And I, poor girl, was dead and gone,
With green grass growing over me.

6. My love is gone, where can he be? (three times)
He no longer gives his love to me.

7. True love, don't weep, true love don't mourn, (three times)
I'm going away from this old town.

New River Train

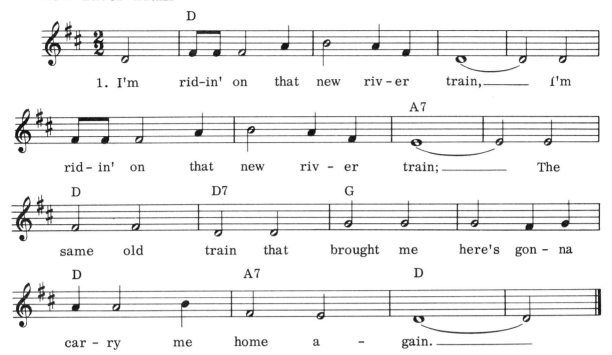

1. I'm rid-in' on that new riv-er train,_____ I'm
rid-in' on that new riv-er train;_____ The
same old train that brought me here's gon-na
car-ry me home a - gain._____

2. Darling, you can't love two, (twice)
   You can't love two, and still to me be true, (etc.)

3. Darling, you can't love three, (twice)
   You can't love three, and still be true to me, (etc.)

4. Darling, you can't love four, (twice)
   You can't love four, and love me any more, (etc.)

5. Darling, you can't love five, (twice)
   You can't love five, and have my love survive, (etc.)

6. Darling, you can't love six, (twice)
   You can't love six, and do those tricks, (etc.)

7. Darling, you can't love seven, (twice)
   You can't love seven, and ever get to heaven, (etc.)

8. Darling, you can't love eight, (twice)
   You can't love eight, and pass the Pearly Gate, (etc.)

9. Darling, you can't love nine, (twice)
   You can't love nine, and still be mine, (etc.)
   (repeat the first verse)

O Hanukkah

SM AND JB

JEWISH FOLK SONG

O Ha-nuk-kah, O Ha-nuk-kah, We greet you with danc-ing,,

This is the time to be gay and ro-manc-ing, come and sing the song of re-

joic-ing and peace, Ha-nuk-kah is here may our joys never cease, And

While we are danc-ing, the can-dles are burn-ing bright.

One for each day we will light on our way, Re-

joic-ing with hearts that are light,   joic-ing with hearts that are light.

Wondrous Love

SOUTHERN U. S.

1. What won-drous love is this, O my soul, O my
soul! What won-drous love is this, O my soul!_____ What
won-drous love is this that caused the Lord_ of bliss To
send this bless-ed gift for my soul, for my soul, To
send this bless-ed gift for my soul:_____

2. When I was sinking down, sinking down, sinking down,
   When I was sinking down, sinking down;
   When I was sinking down beneath God's righteous frown,
   Christ laid aside His crown for my soul, for my soul,
   Christ laid aside His crown for my soul.

3. And when from death I'm free, I'll sing on, I'll sing on,
   And when from death I'm free, I'll sing on;
   And when from death I'm free, I'll sing and joyful be,
   And through eternity I'll sing on, I'll sing on,
   And through eternity I'll sing on.

Loch Lomond

SCOTLAND

1. By___ yon bon-nie banks and by yon bon-nie braes, Where the
sun shines bright on Loch Lo - mond, Where me and my true love were
ev-er wont to gae, On the bon-nie, bon-nie banks of Loch Lo - mond.

Chorus

Oh! ye'll take the high road, and I'll take the low road, And
I'll be in Scot-land a - fore ye, But me and my true love we'll
nev-er meet a - gain On the bon-nie, bon-nie banks of Loch Lo - mond.

2. 'Twas there that we parted in yon shady glen
On the steep, steep side of Ben Lomond,
Where in purple hue the highland hills we
    view,
And the moon coming out in the gloaming.

3. The wee birdies sing, and the wild flowers
    spring,
And in sunshine the waters are sleeping,
But the broken hearts kens nae second spring
    again,
Though the waeful may cease frae their greet-
    ing.

Beautiful Homeland

TURKEY

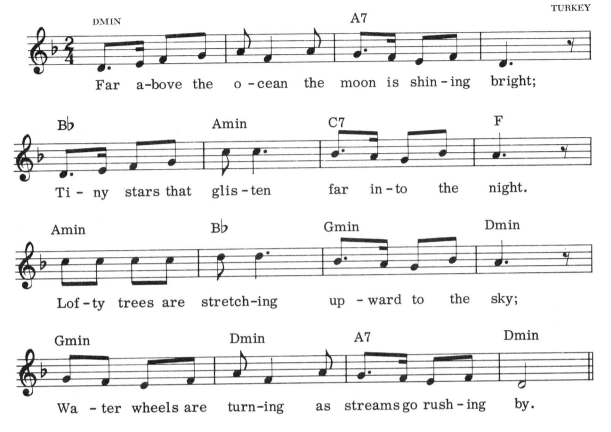

Far a-bove the o-cean the moon is shin-ing bright;

Ti - ny stars that glis-ten far in-to the night.

Lof-ty trees are stretch-ing up - ward to the sky;

Wa - ter wheels are turn-ing as streams go rush-ing by.

—Melody by Ali Ulvi Baradan, Izmir, Turkey. Used by permission. Words by Sally Monsour.

One More River
(NOAH'S ARK)

SPIRITUAL

1. Old No-ah built him-self an ark, There's one more riv-er to cross, And built it all of hick-o-ry bark, There's one more riv-er to cross.____

Chorus One more riv-er,____ And that's the riv-er of Jor-dan; One more riv-er,____ There's one more riv-er to cross.____

2. The animals came two by two, there's one more river to cross,
   The elephant and kangaroo, there's one more river to cross.

3. The animals came three by three, there's one more river to cross,
   The baboon and the chimpanzee, there's one more river to cross.

4. The animals came four by four, there's one more river to cross,
   Old Noah got mad and hollered for more, there's one more river to cross.

5. The animals came five by five, there's one more river to cross,
   The bees came swarming from the hive, there's one more river to cross.

6. The animals came six by six, there's one more river to cross,
   The lion laughed at the monkey's tricks, there's one more river to cross.

7. When Noah found he had no sail, there's one more river to cross,
   He just ran up his old coat tail, there's one more river to cross.

8. Before the voyage did begin, there's one more river to cross.
   Old Noah pulled the gangplank in, there's one more river to cross.

9. They never knew where they were at, there's one more river to cross,
   'Til the old ark bumped on Ararat, there's one more river to cross.

Lone Star Trail

U. S. COWBOY

1. I start-ed on the trail on June twen-ty-third, I've been punch-ing Tex-as cat-tle on the Lone Star Trail;

Chorus

Sing-ing ki - yi yip - pi yap - pi yay, yap - pi yay! Sing - ing ki - yi yip - pi yap - pi yay.

2. I'm up in the morning long before daylight,
   And before I'm sleeping the moon is shining bright, etc.

3. My feet are in the stirrups and my rope is at my side,
   And I never yet have seen the horse that I can't ride, etc.

4. Oh, it's bacon and beans about every day,
   And I'd just about as soon be eating prairie hay, etc.

5. Now my seat is in the saddle, and my hand is on my rope,
   And my eye is on the dogies, I'm a good cow poke, etc.

6. With my knees in the saddle and my seat in the sky,
   I'll continue punching cattle in the sweet by and by, etc.

Waterbound

NORTH CAROLINA TRADITIONAL

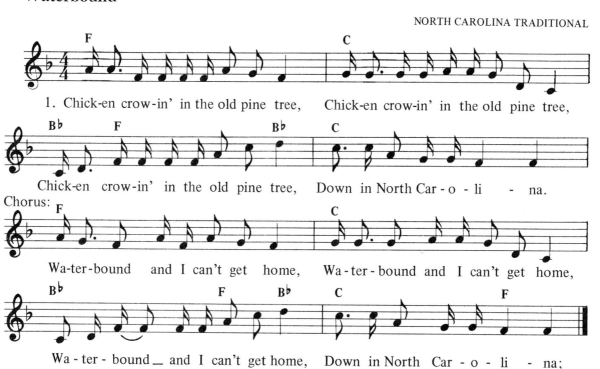

1. Chick-en crow-in' in the old pine tree, Chick-en crow-in' in the old pine tree,

Chick-en crow-in' in the old pine tree, Down in North Car - o - li - na.

Chorus:

Wa-ter-bound and I can't get home, Wa-ter-bound and I can't get home,

Wa - ter - bound and I can't get home, Down in North Car - o - li - na;

2. I'm goin' home with the one I love.
3. Old man's mad and I don't care.
4. Wheelbarrow's sittin' in the old cow shed.

As published by World Around Songs, Burnsville, N.C. Used by permission.

Silvery Star

ARR. AUGUSTUS A. ZANZIG

ITALIAN FOLK SONG

ENGLISH TRANS. BY MAX EXNER

I looked up in the star-light one night when I was lone - ly; One

star of all the stars there was our star on - ly.

From *Tent and Trail Songs*. Copyright 1962, World Around Songs. Used by permission.

Hallelu

TRINIDAD FOLK SONG

1. Sing to _ the mu-sic,   Hal - le-lu, _ (Clap) Sing to _ the mu-sic,   Hal - le-lu, _ (Clap)
   La la _ la la la,   Hal - le-lu, _ (Clap) La la _ la la la,   Hal - le-lu, _ (Clap)

   Sing to _ the mu - sic,   Hal - le - lu, _ (Clap) Sing to _ the mu-sic,   Hal - le-lu. _ (Clap)
   La la _ la la la,   Hal - le - lu, _ (Clap) La la _ la la la,   Hal - le-lu. _ (Clap)

2. Move with the music, . . . (etc.)
   La la la la la, . . . (etc.)

Simple Gifts

Pop Goes the Weasel

ENGLISH SINGING GAME

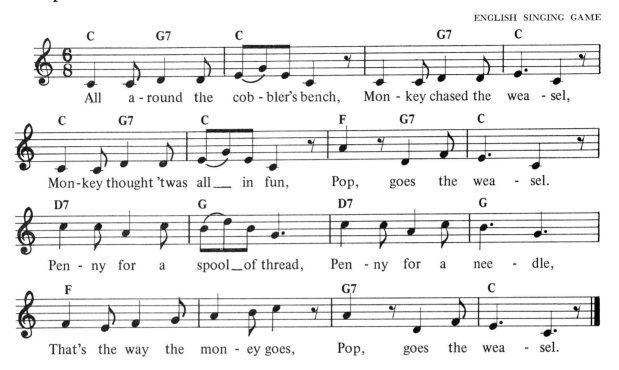

All a-round the cob-bler's bench, Mon-key chased the wea-sel,

Mon-key thought 'twas all __ in fun, Pop, goes the wea-sel.

Pen-ny for a spool __ of thread, Pen-ny for a nee-dle,

That's the way the mon-ey goes, Pop, goes the wea-sel.

Night Herding Song

LIKE A LULLABY

COWBOY SONG

Go slow lit-tle dog-gies quit mov-in' a-round, I'm

tired of your ramb-lin' all o-ver the ground, Go slow lit-tle dog-gies, go

slow. _____ Hi - o, Hi - o Hi - o. _____

Peace Like a River

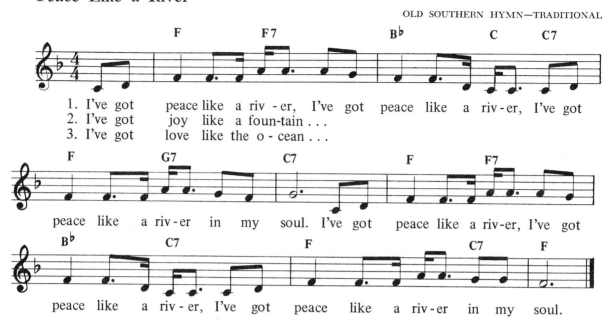

OLD SOUTHERN HYMN—TRADITIONAL

1. I've got   peace like a riv-er, I've got peace like a riv-er, I've got
2. I've got   joy like a foun-tain . . .
3. I've got   love like the o-cean . . .

peace like a riv-er in my soul. I've got   peace like a riv-er, I've got

peace like a riv-er, I've got   peace like a riv-er in my soul.

Hevenu Shalom

JEWISH

He-ve-nu sha-lom a lei-chem, __ He-ve-nu

sha — lom a lei-chem, __ He-ve-ny sha — lom a

lei - chem, __ He-ve-nu sha - lom, sha -lom, sha - lom a lei - chem.

"Peace to all of us"—Translation
Pronunciation—Hay-vay-nee shah-loam ah-lay-khem

A version of this song may be found on "Israeli Songs for Children," Folkways Records, FC 7226.

Down the River

PLAY PARTY SONG

RIVER CHANTEY

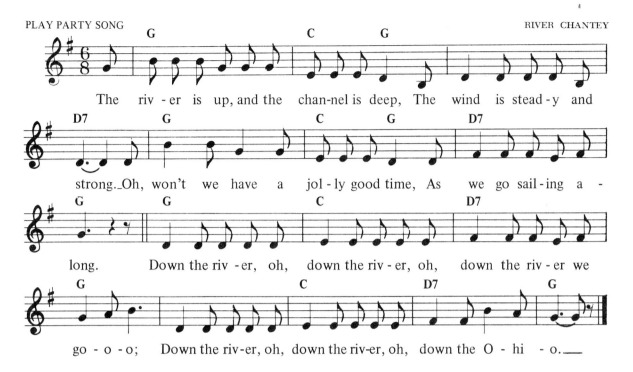

The riv-er is up, and the chan-nel is deep, The wind is stead-y and strong._Oh, won't we have a jol-ly good time, As we go sail-ing a-long. Down the riv-er, oh, down the riv-er, oh, down the riv-er we go-o-o; Down the riv-er, oh, down the riv-er, oh, down the O-hi-o.___

This rollicking song has often been sung while the reel is danced, as in the Virginia Reel.

Cape Cod Chantey

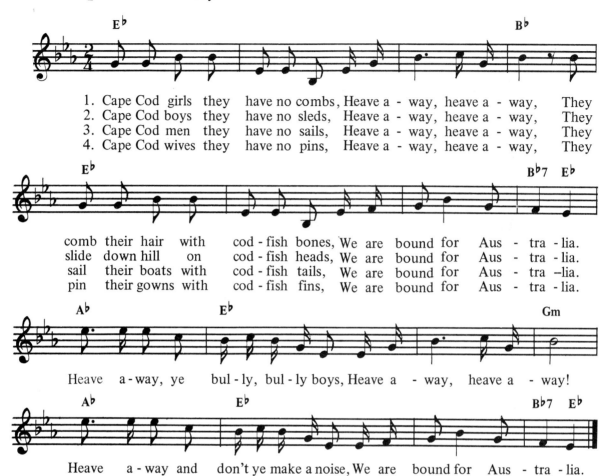

1. Cape Cod girls they have no combs, Heave a - way, heave a - way, They
2. Cape Cod boys they have no sleds, Heave a - way, heave a - way, They
3. Cape Cod men they have no sails, Heave a - way, heave a - way, They
4. Cape Cod wives they have no pins, Heave a - way, heave a - way, They

comb their hair with cod - fish bones, We are bound for Aus - tra - lia.
slide down hill on cod - fish heads, We are bound for Aus - tra - lia.
sail their boats with cod - fish tails, We are bound for Aus - tra –lia.
pin their gowns with cod - fish fins, We are bound for Aus - tra - lia.

Heave a - way, ye bul - ly, bul - ly boys, Heave a - way, heave a - way!

Heave a - way and don't ye make a noise, We are bound for Aus - tra - lia.

My Home's in Montana

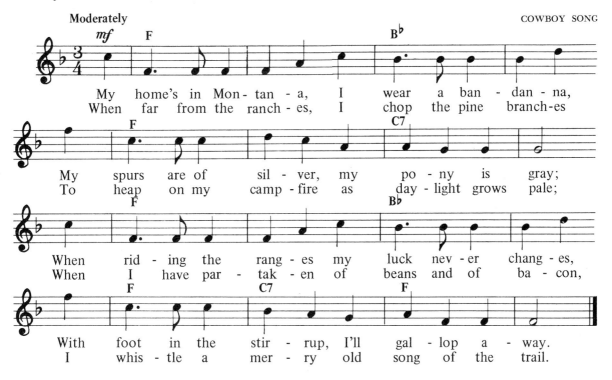

Little Tom Tinker

Lovely Evening
(Three part round)

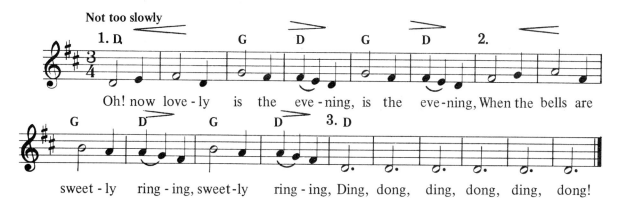

Oh! now love-ly is the eve-ning, is the eve-ning, When the bells are sweet-ly ring-ing, sweet-ly ring-ing, Ding, dong, ding, dong, ding, dong!

Haida

Hai-da Hai-da Hai-da Hai-da Hai-da Hai-da Hai-da

Hai-da Hai-da Hai-da Hai-da Hai-da Hai-da Hai-da

The word "Haida" does not mean anything.
Chassidim is a sect of Eastern European Jews who celebrate God with singing and dancing.

Kindness of Shelley Gordon. Used by permission.

Lullaby Round

ANONYMOUS

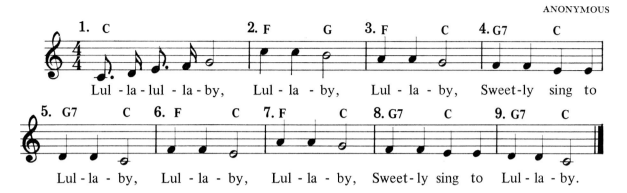

As found in *Rounds,* World Around Songs, Burnsville, N. C. Used by permission.

The Cost of Gladness

ENGLISH BY MAX EXNER

SWEDISH GERMAN ROUND

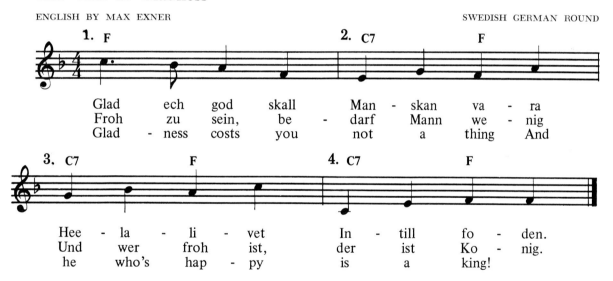

As found in *Rounds,* World Around Songs, Burnsville, N. C. Used by permission.

Jacob's Ladder

SPIRITUAL

1. We are climb-ing Ja - cob's lad - der, We are climb - ing Ja - cob's lad - der, We are climb - ing Ja - cob's lad - der sol - diers of the cross.———

2. Every round goes higher, higher, etc.
3. Brother, do you love my Jesus? etc.
4. If you love Him, you must serve Him, etc.
5. We are climbing higher, higher, etc.

Las Mañanitas

Estas son las mañanitas que cantaba el Rey David,
Pero no eran tanbonitas como las cantan aquí.
Despierta, mi bién, despierta, mira que ya amaneció;
Ya los pajarillos cantan, la luna ya se metió.
Despierta, mi bién, despierta, mira que ya amaneció;
Ya los pajarillos cantan, la luma ya se metió.
Estas son las mañanitas que cantaba el Rey David,
Pero no eran tanbonitas como las cantan aquí.

appendix A.
general sources on recreation and leisure

ARNOLD, N. D. *The Interrelated Arts in Leisure.* St. Louis: The C. V. Mosby Company, 1976.

BANNON, JOSEPH J. *Leisure Resources: Its Comprehensive Planning.* Englewood Cliffs, N. J.: Prentice-Hall, Inc., 1976.

BUCHER, CHARLES A., and RICHARD D. BUCHER. *Recreation for Today's Society.* Englewood Cliffs, N. J.: Prentice-Hall, Inc., 1971.

CARGHER, J. *Music for Pleasure.* Sydney: Ure Smith, 1970.

CARLSON, R. E.; T. R. DEPPE, and J. R. MacLEAN. *Recreation in American Life,* Second Edition. Belmont, Calif.: Wadsworth Publishing Co., Inc., 1972.

CHEEK, NEIL H., and W. R. BURCH. *The Social Organization of Leisure in Human Society.* New York: Harper and Row, 1976.

CHEEK, NEIL H.; JR.; DONALD R. FIELD; and RABEL J. BURDGE. *Leisure and Recreation Places.* Ann Arbor: Ann Arbor Science Publishers, Inc., 1976.

Coming To Our Senses. The Arts, Education and Americans Panel. New York: McGraw-Hill Book Company, 1977.

FARRELL, P., and LUNDGREN, H. *The Process of Recreational Programming.* New York: John Wiley and Sons, 1978.

GASTON, E. T. *Music in Therapy.* New York: Macmillan Publishing Co., Inc., 1968.

A Guide to Books in Recreation. 14th annual edition. Washington, D. C.: National Recreation and Park Association, 1971.

HOPKINS, J. *A Book of American Music Celebrations, Festival!* New York: Macmillan Publishing Co., Inc., 1969.

Journal of Leisure Research. Published annually by the National Recreation and Park Association, Washington, D. C.

KRAUS, R. *Recreation and Leisure in Modern Society.* Englewood Cliffs, N. J.: Prentice-Hall, Inc., 1971.

MULAC, M. E. *Hobbies, The Creative Use of Leisure.* New York: Harper and Row, Publishers, 1959.

MURPHY, JAMES F. *Recreation and Leisure Service: A Humanistic Perspective.* Dubuque, Iowa: Wm. C. Brown Company Publishers, 1975.

ROBERTS, J. S. *Black Music of Two Worlds.* New York: Praeger Publishers, 1972.

ROBINSON, J. P. *How Americans Use Time.* New York: Praeger Publishers, 1977.

VANNIER, M. H. *Methods and Materials in Recreation Leadership.* Second Edition, Philadelphia: W. B. Saunders Co., 1977.

WEISKOPF, DONALD C. *A Guide to Recreation and Leisure.* Boston: Allyn and Bacon, Inc., 1975.

appendix B.
selected books about music for libraries and recreation centers

I. *For Young People*

The following books are generally suited for young readers in pre-teen and early-teen years.

ALEXANDER, MELVIN. *Sound Science.* Englewood Cliffs, N. J.: Prentice-Hall, 1970.

APEL, WILLI, and DANIEL, RALPH. *The Harvard Brief Dictionary of Music.* Cambridge, Mass.: Harvard University Press, 1960.

ATTAWAY, WILLIAM. *Hear America Singing.* Introduction by Harry Belafonte. New York: Lion, 1968.

BALET, JAN. *What Makes an Orchestra.* New York: Oxford, 1951.

BALLIETT, WHITNEY. *Dinosaurs in the Morning.* Philadelphia: J. B. Lippincott, Co., 1962. (Description of Jazz).

BERNSTEIN, LEONARD. *The Joy of Music.* New York: Simon and Schuster, 1959.

————. *Young Peoples Concerts for Reading and Listening.* New York: Simon and Schuster, 1962. (Book and five 7-inch 33 1/3 recordings.)

BERNSTEIN, SHIRLEY. *Making Music: Leonard Bernstein.* Chicago: Encyclopedia Brittanica, 1963.

BRITTEN, BENJAMIN, and IMOGENE HOLST. *Wonderful World of Music.* Garden City, New York: David McKay Co., Inc., rev. 1969.

BROWNE, CHARLES A. Rev. by Willard Heaps, *The Story of Our National Ballads.* New York: Crowell, 1960.

BULLA, CLYDE. *Stories of Favorite Operas.* New York: Crowell, 1959.

CHISSELL, JOAN. *Chopin.* New York: Crowell, 1965.

COKER, JERRY. *The Jazz Idiom.* New York: Prentice-Hall, 1975.

COLLIER, JAMES. *Which Musical Instrument Shall I Play?* New York: Grosset and Dunlap, 1969.

CRAIG, JEAN. *The Story of Musical Notes.* New York: Lerner Pub., 1962.

CROSS, MILTON, and JOHN and DAVID EWEN. *Encyclopedia of the Great Composers and Their Music.* rev. New York: Doubleday, 1962.

CUNNINGHAM, DALE. *Picture Book of Music and Its Makers.* New York: Sterling, 1963.

DACHS, DAVID. *Encyclopedia of Pop/Rock.* New York: Scholastic Book Service, 1972.

DAVIS, MARILYN, and ARNOLD BROIDO. *Music Dictionary.* rev. New York: Doubleday, 1956.

DEITZ, BETTY, and MICHAEL OLATUNJI. *Musical Instruments of Africa,* (with 7 inch record). New York: John Day, 1965.

DUFF, MAGGIE. *Jonny and His Drum.* New York: Henry Z. Walck, 1972.

ERLICH, LILLIAN. *What Is Jazz All About?* New York: Messner, 1962.

EWEN, DAVID, and LEONARD BERNSTEIN. *A Biography for Young People.* Philadelphia: Chilton, 1965.

FISHER, RENEE. *Musical Prodigies.* New York: Association Press, 1973.

Fox, Lilla M. *Instruments of Popular Music.* New York: Roy, 1968.

Frost, Frances. *Amahl and the Night Visitors.* New York: McGraw-Hill Book Co., Inc., 1952.

Gollomb, Joseph. *Albert Schweitzer, Genius of the Jungle.* New York: Vanguard, 1949.

Gough, Catherine. *Boyhoods of Great Composers.* Books 1 and 2. New York: Walck, 1961, 1965.

Hughes, Langston. *Famous Negro Music Makers.* New York: Dodd, Mead, 1955.

———. *First Book of Jazz.* New York: Watts, 1955.

Kauffman, Helen L. *The Story of Haydn.* New York: Grosset and Dunlap, 1962.

Keepnews, Orrin, and Bill Grauer. *Pictorial History of Jazz.* New York: Crown, 1955.

Kellogg, Charlotte H. *Paderewski.* New York: Viking, 1956.

Kert, Russell, and Taylor, Deems. Compiled by Rupert Hughes. *Music Lovers' Encyclopedia.* New York: Garden City, 1954.

Lerner, Sharon. *Places of Musical Fame.* Minneapolis, Minn.: Lerner Pub., 1967.

Lingg, Ann M. *John Philip Sousa.* New York: Holt, 1954.

Machlis, Joseph. *American Composers of Our Time.* New York: Crowell, 1963.

Maynard, Olga. *The Ballet Companion.* Philadelphia: Macrae Smith, 1957.

McGhee, Thomasine, and Alice Nelson. *People and Music.* Boston: Allyn and Bacon, Inc., 1963.

McLin, Lena. *Pulse: A History of Music.* Park Ridge, Ill.: Neil A. Kjos Music Co., 1977.

McMillaw, Bruce. *The Alphabet Symphony.* New York: William Morrow & Co., 1977.

Posell, Elsa. *American Composers.* Boston: Houghton Mifflin, 1963.

Power-Waters, Alma S. *Melody Maker.* New York: Dutton, 1959. (The life of Sir Arthur Sullivan.)

Richardson, Allen. *Tooters, Tweeters, Strings and Beaters.* New York: Grosset and Dunlap, 1964.

Rublonsky, John. *Popular Music.* New York: Basic Books, Inc., 1967.

Shippen, Katherine, and Anca Seidlova. *The Heritage of Music.* New York: Viking, 1963.

Slonimsky, Nicholas. *The Road to Music.* rev. New York: Dodd, Mead, 1966.

Sootin, Harry. *Science Experiments with Sound.* New York: W. W. Norton, 1964.

Spier, Peter. *Crash! Bang! Boom!* New York: Doubleday, 1972.

———. *The Erie Canal.* New York: Doubleday, 1970.

Stambler, Irwin. *The Worlds of Sound.* New York: W. W. Norton, 1967.

Stoddard, Hope. *From These Come Music.* New York: Crowell, 1962.

Terkel, Studs. *Giants of Jazz.* New York: Crowell, 1957.

Thomas, Henry, and Dana Lee Thomas. *Living Biographies of Great Composers.* New York: 1959.

Thompson, Ross. *A Noisy Book.* New York: Scroll Press, Inc., 1971.

Ulanov, Barry. *Handbook of Jazz.* New York: Viking, 1957.

Ulrich, Homer. *Famous Women Singers.* New York: Dodd, Mead, 1956.

II. For Adults

The following books are suitable for adult reading and reference. The list is highly selective.

Anderson, Marian. *My Lord, What a Morning.* New York: Viking, 1958. (An autobiography.)

Apel, Willi. *Harvard Brief Dictionary of Music.* Cambridge, Mass.: Harvard University Press, 1960.

Attaway, William. *Hear America Sing.* New York: Lion, 1968.

Broekema, Andrew J. *The Music Listener.* Dubuque, Iowa: Wm. C. Brown Co., 1978.

Caruso, Dorothy. *Enrico Caruso.* New York: Simon and Schuster, 1945.

Choate, Robert, and Nick Rossi. *Music of Our Time.* Boston: Crescendo Publishing, 1970.

Cohn, Nik. *Rock from the Beginning.* New York: Stein and Day, 1969.

Copland, Aaron. *What to Listen for in Music.* New York: McGraw-Hill, 1939.

Cross, Milton. *New Complete Stories of Great Operas.* rev. New York: Doubleday, 1955.

———, and David Ewen. *Encyclopedia of the Great Composers and Their Music.* rev. New York: Doubleday, 1962.

Ewen, David. *The Story of Arturo Toscanini.* New York: Holt, 1960.

Hentoff, Nat. *Jazz Country.* New York: Harper and Row, 1965. (A must for those interested in Jazz.)

HOFFER, CHARLES. *The Understanding of Music,* 4th ed. Belmont, Calif.: Wadsworth Publishing Co., 1981.

JAMES, BURNETT. *An Adventure in Music.* Boston: Crescendo Publishing, n.d. (Simple adventure story about a man with polio and his experiences with music.)

JONES, LeROI. *Black Music.* New York: William Morrow, 1971.

KERMAN, JOSEPH. *Listen,* 3rd ed. New York: Worth Publishers, Inc., 1980.

MACHLIS, JOSEPH. *Introduction to Contemporary Music.* New York: W. W. Norton, 1961.

———. *Music Adventures in Listening.* New York: W. W. Norton, 1968.

MILLER, HUGH. *Introduction to Music Appreciation.* New York: Chilton Co., 1961.

OLIVER, PAUL. *The Story of the Blues.* New York: Chilton Press, 1969.

POLITOSKE, DANIEL. *Music,* 2nd ed. Englewood Cliffs, N. J.: Prentice-Hall, Inc., 1979.

ROREM, NED. *Music and People.* New York: George Braziller, 1968.

RUBLOWSKY, JOHN. *Black Music in America.* New York: Basic Books, 1971.

SHAW, ARNOLD. *The Rock Revolution.* London: Collier and Macmillan Ltd., 1969.

SOUTHERN, EILEEN. *The Music of Black Americans: A History.* New York: W. W. Norton, 1971.

STAMBLER, IRWIN. *The Worlds of Sound.* New York: W. W. Norton, Inc., 1967.

THOMPSON, OSCAR. *How to Understand Music.* New York: Fawcett Publishers, 1958.

ULANOV, BARRY. *Handbook of Jazz.* New York: Viking, 1957.

ULRICH, HOMER. *Famous Women Singers.* New York: Dodd, Mead, 1956.

appendix C.
sources on rhythms, movement, and dancing

Sources on Rhythms, Movement, and Dancing

I. BOOKS

ANDREWS, GLADYS. *Creative Rhythmic Movement for Children.* Englewood Cliffs, New Jersey: Prentice-Hall, Inc., 1954.

ATHEY, MARGARET, and GWEN HOTCHKISS. *A Galaxy of Games for the Music Class.* West Nyack, New York: Parker Publishing Co., Inc., 1975.

BOORMAN, JOYCE. *Creative Dance in Grades Four to Six.* Don Mills, Ontario, Canada: Longman Canada Limited, 1971.

CHERRY, CLARE. *Creative Movement for the Developing Child.* Revised edition. Belmont, California: Fearon Publishers, Inc., 1971.

COHEN, MARILYN; PATRICIA LINDELL; and SALLY MONSOUR. *Rhythm in Music and Dance for Children.* Belmont, California: Wadsworth Publishing Co., 1966.

CREWS, DR. KATHERINE. *Music and Perceptual-Motor Development.* New York: The Center for Applied Research in Education, Inc., 1975.

DOLL, EDNA, and MARY JARMAN NELSON. *Rhythms Today.* Morristown, New Jersey: Silver Burdett Co., 1964.

DORIAN, MARGERY, and FRANCES GULLAND. *Telling Stories Through Movement.* Belmont, California: Fearon Publishers, Inc., 1974.

DROUILLARD, RICHARD, and SHERRY RAYNOR. *Move It! ! !.* Washington, D. C.: AAHPER, 1977.

EXINER, JOHANNA. *Teaching Creative Movement.* Boston: Plays, Inc., 1974.

FLEMING, GLADYS ANDREWS, editor. *Children's Dance.* Washington, D. C.: AAHPER, 1973.

FLEMING, GLADYS ANDREWS. *Creative Rhythmic Movement.* Englewood Cliffs, New Jersey: Prentice-Hall, Inc., 1976.

FOWLER, JOHN, and CAROLYN J. RASMUS, editors. *Movement Activities for Places and Spaces.* Washington, D. C.: AAHPER, 1977.

GELL, HEATHER. *Music Movement and the Young Child.* Revised edition. Sydney, Australia: Australasian Publishing Co., 1973.

GRAY, VERA, and RACHEL PERCIVAL. *Music, Movement, and Mime.* New York: Oxford Publishing Co., 1965.

HALPRIN, ANNA. *Movement Ritual.* San Francisco Dancers' Workshop, 1979.

Handy Book of Folk Dances World Around Songs, Burnsville, North Carolina 28714.

HAYES, ELIZABETH R. *Introduction to the Teaching of Dance.* New York: The Ronald Press Co., 1964.

HIGHWATER, JAMAKE. *Ritual of the Wind.* New York: The Viking Press, 1977.

HOOD, MARGUERITE V. *Teaching Rhythm and Using Classroom Instruments.* Englewood Cliffs, N. J.: Prentice-Hall, Inc., 1964.

HUET, MICHEL. *The Dance, Art and Ritual of Africa.* New York: Pantheon Books, 1978.

HUMPHREYS, LOUISE, and JERROLD ROSS. *Interpreting Music Through Movement.* Englewood Cliffs, N. J.: Prentice-Hall, Inc., 1964.

IMEL, E. CARMEN, editor. *Focus on Dance: VIII, Dance Heritage.* Washington, D. C.: AAHPER, 1977.

JONES, BESSIE, and BESS LOMAX HAWES. *Step It Down.* New York: Harper & Row, 1972.

JONES, GENEVIEVE. *Seeds of Movement.* Pittsburgh, Pennsylvania: Volkwein Bros., Inc., 1971.

JOYCE, MARY. *First Steps in Teaching Creative Dance to Children.* Second Edition. Palo Alto, California: Mayfield Publishing Co., 1980.

McGHEE, JOANNE, and SALLY MONSOUR. *Movement Experiences in the Primary Curriculum.* Fort Worth, Texas: Harris Music Publications, 1978.

MURDOCK, ELIZABETH B. *Expressive Movement.* Edinburgh and London: W & R Chambers, 1973.

NELSON, ESTHER L. *Movement Games for Children of All Ages.* New York: Sterling Publishing Co., Ltd., 1975.

NORTH, MARION. *Body Movement for Children.* Boston: Plays, Inc., 1972.

ROSENSTRAUCH, HENRIETTA. *Percussion Rhythm Music Movement.* Pittsburgh, Pennsylvania: Volkwein Bros., Inc., 1970.

RUSSELL, JOAN. *Creative Dance in the Primary School.* Estover, Plymouth, G. B.: MacDonald and Evans Ltd., second edition, 1975.

SIEGEL, MARCIA B. *The Shapes of Change.* Boston: Houghton Mifflin, 1979.

SLATER, WENDY. *Teaching Modern Educational Dance.* Estover, Plymouth, G. B.: MacDonald and Evans Ltd., 1974.

Square Dance. World Around Songs, Burnsville, North Carolina 28714.

STECHER, MIRIAM B., and HUGH McELHENY. *Music and Movement Improvisations.* New York: MacMillan Publishing Co., 1972.

TAYLOR, CARLA. *Rhythm.* Palo Alto, California: Peek Publications, 1974.

WETHERED, AUDREY G. *Drama and Movement in Therapy.* London: MacDonald and Evans Ltd., 1973.

II. RECORDINGS

All the following records may be ordered using the number listed, from the Educational Record Center, 3120 Maple Drive, N.E., Suite 124, Atlanta, Georgia 30305.

Activity and Game Songs for Children. Tom Glazer. Vol. II, #658; Vol. III, #687.
Bean Bag Activities. Jill Gallina. Kimbe Records, KIM 7055.
Call-and-Response Rhythmic Group Singing. Ella Jenkins, R 7638.
Children's Dances Without Partners. Vol. 1, #2809; Vol 2, #3019.
Coordination Skills. Kimbo Records, KEA 6050.
Dances Without Partners. "Buzz" Glass, #46.
Get Ready to Square Dance. Jack Capon and Rosemary Hallum, Ph.D., #68.
Kids Action Songs, B 56.
Modern American Square Dance Series. Kimbo Records, Vol. I, KIM 4060; Vol. II, KIM 5080; Vol. III, KM 8070.
Move Along Alphabet. Kimbo Records, KIM 0510.
Movement Fun, #21.
Music for Creative Movement. Kimbo Records, KIM 6070-80.
Music for Movement Exploration. Kimbo Records, KIM 5090.
Perceptual Motor Activities. Kimbo Records, KIM 9078.
Perceptual-Motor Rhythm Games. Jack Capon and Rosemary Hallum, Ph.D., #50.
Playtime Parachute Fun. Jill Gallina. Kimbo Records, KIM 7056.

Rhythm Band for Little People. Kimbo Records, KIM 0840.
Rhythms of Childhood. Ella Jenkins, R 7653.
Rhythm Stick Activities. LP/Guide, #55; Cassette/Guide, C 55.
Rope Activities, #64.
Simplified Lummi Stick Activities. Kimbo Records,, KIM 2015.
Square Dance Fun for Everyone. Kimbo Records, KEA 1138.
Streamer and Rhythm Activities. Henry "Buzz" Glass and Jack Capon, AR 578.
Swing Your Partner, #74.
This Is Rhythm. Ella Jenkins, R 7652.
To Move Is to Be. Kimbo Records, KEA 8060.

appendix D.
classified listing of musical resources

AUDIO-VISUAL AIDS EQUIPMENT

Audio House, 307 E. 9th St., Lawrence, Kan. 6604

Bowmar Records, Inc., 622 Rodier Drive, Glendale, Calif. 91201

Stanley Bowmar Co., Inc., 4 Broadway, Valhalla, N.Y. 10595

Century Records Mfg. Co.—Century Custom Recording Service, P.O. Box 308, Squgus, Calif. 91350

Chesterfield Music Shops, Inc., 12 Warren St., New York, N.Y. 10007

Children's Music Center, Inc., 5373 West Pico Blvd., Los Angeles, Calif. 90019

Crest Records, Inc., 220 Broadway, Huntington Station, N.Y. 11746

Custom Fidelity Record Co., 222 E. Glenarm St., Pasadena, Calif. 91101

Folkways Records, 43 W. 61st St., New York, N.Y. 10023

Herco Products, Inc., 53 W. 23rd St., New York, N.Y. 10010

Ken-Del Productions, Inc., Custom Record Division, 111 Valley Road—Richardson Park, Wilmington, Del. 19804

RCA Records, 1133 Ave. of the Americas, New York, N.Y. 10036

Radio-Matic of America, Inc., 760 Ramsey Ave., Hillside, N.J. 07205

Society for Visual Education, Inc., 1345 Diversey Parkway, Chicago, Ill. 60614

Vogt Quality Recordings, P.O. Box 302, Needham, Mass. 02192

BAND & ORCHESTRA INSTRUMENT MANUFACTURERS

W. T. Armstrong Company, Inc., 1000 Industrial Pkway, Elkhart, Ind., 46516

Artley, Inc., P.O. Box 2280, Nogales, Ariz. 85621

C. Bruno & Son, Inc., 55 Marcus Drive, Melville, N.Y. 11746
3443 E. Commerce St., San Antonio, Texas 78206
5720 Union Pacific Ave., Los Angeles, Calif. 90022

Conn Corporation, 2520 Industrial Pkway, Elkhart, Ind. 46514

Fender Musical Instruments, CBS Musical Instruments, 1300 East Valencia, Fullerton, Calif. 92631

Fox Products Corp., South Whitley, Ind. 46787

K. G. Gemeinhardt Co., Inc., P.O. Box 788, Rt. 19, South Elkhart, Ind., 46515

Getzen Company, Inc., 211 W. Centralia St., Elkhorn, Wis. 53121

Goya Music, Div. of Avnet, Inc., 53 W. 23rd St., New York, N.Y. 10010

Wm. R. Gratz, Co., Inc., 14 Bixley Heath, Lynbrook, N.Y. 11563

The Fred Gretsch Co., Inc., 60 Broadway, Brooklyn, N.Y. 11211

Hargail Music, Inc., 157 W. 57th St., New York, N.Y. 10019

G. C. Jenkins Co., P.O. Box 2221, Decatur, Ill. 62526

Kelischek Workshop for Historical Instruments, 386 Allendale Drive, S.E., Atlanta, Ga. 30317
King Musical Instruments, 33999 Curtis Blvd., Eastlake, Ohio 44094
G. LeBlanc Corporation, 7019 30th Ave., Kenosha, Wis. 53141
William Lewis & Sons, 7390 N. Lincoln Ave., Lincolnwood, Ill. 60646
The Linton Company Inc., 711 Middleton Run Road, Elkhart, Ind. 46514
Ludwig Industries, 1728 N. Damen Ave., Chicago, Ill. 60647
Martin Band Instruments, DeKalb, Ill. 60115
Meinl-Weston Musical Instrument Company, 35 N. Ayer St., Harvard, Ill. 60033
C. Meisel Music Co., Subsidiary of Avnet, Inc., 2332 Morris Ave., Union, N. J. 07083
Mirafone Corporation, P.O. Box 909 Sun Valley, Calif. 91352
Musser-Kitching—Div. Ludwig Industries, 505 Shawest, La Grange, Ill. 60525
F. E. Olds & Son, Inc., 350 S. Raymond Ave., Fullerton, Calif. 92631
Polisi Bassoon Corp., 244 W. 49th Street, New York, N.Y. 10019
G. Pruefer Mfg. Co., Inc., 185 Union Avenue, Providence, R. I. 02909
F. A. Reynolds Co., 5520 N. First Street, Abilene, Texas 79603
Rogers Drums, CBS Musical Instruments, 1300 East Valencia, Fullerton, California 92631
Walter E. Sear, 118 West 57th Street, New York, N.Y. 10019
Selmer—Division of Magnovox, Box 310, Elkhart, Indiana 46515
Scherl & Roth Incorporated, 1729 Superior Avenue, Cleveland, Ohio 44114
Schilke Music Products, Inc., 529 S. Wabash Avenue, Chicago, Illinois 60605
Slingerland Drum Co., 6633 N. Milwaukee Avenue, Niles, Illinois 60648
Vincent Bach Corp., 1119 N. Main, Box 377, Elkhart, Indiana 46514
Avedis Zildjian Company, P.O. Box 198 Accord, Mass. 02018

BAND UNIFORM AND CHOIR GOWN MANUFACTURERS

Bandribbons, Monmouth, Oregon 97361
Collegiate Cap and Gown Company, 1000 No. Market Street, Champaign, Ill. 61820
DeMoulin Bros. & Co., 1083 S. Fourth, Greenville, Illinois 62246
The Fechheimer Bros. Co., 4545 Malsbary Road, Cincinnati, Ohio 45242
Sol Frank Uniforms, Inc., 702 South Santa Rosa St., San Antonio, Texas 78207
Fruhauf Southwest Uniform Company, 312 East English Street, Wichita, Kansas 67202
Robert Rollins Blazers, Inc., 242 Park Avenue, South, New York, N.Y. 10003
"Uniforms By Ostwald," Inc., Ostwald Plaza, Box No. 70, Staten Island, New York 10314
The C. E. Ward Company, New London, Conn. 44851

MUSIC TEXTBOOK PUBLISHERS

Allyn and Bacon, Inc., 470 Atlantic Avenue, Boston Mass. 02210
American Book Company, 135 W. 50th Street, N.Y. 10020
Appleton-Century-Crofts, Educational Division of Meredith Corp., 440 Park Avenue, South, New York, N.Y. 10016
William C. Brown Company Publishers, 2460 Kerper Blvd., Dubuque, Iowa 52001
Follett Educational Corporation, 1010 W. Washington Blvd., Chicago, Illinois 60607
Ginn and Company, Statler Building, Boston, Mass. 02117
Holt, Rinehart and Winston, Inc., 383 Madison Avenue, New York, New York 10017
Macmillan Publishing, 866 3rd Ave., N.Y. 10022
Prentice-Hall, Inc., Englewood Cliffs, N. J. 07632
Silver-Burdett Co., Morristown, New Jersey 07960
Wadsworth Publishing Company, Inc., 10 Davis Drive, Belmont, California 94002

MUSICAL EQUIPMENT MANUFACTURERS

Bela Seating Company, Inc., 9505 South Prairie Avenue, Chicago, Illinois 60628

Clarin Corporation, 4640 West Harrison Street, Chicago, Illinois 60644

The Empire Music Company, Ltd., 934–12th Street, New Westminster, B. C., Canada

Krauth and Benninghofen, Inc., 3001 Symmes Road, Hamilton, Ohio 45012

Lyons, 530 Riverview Ave., Elkhart, Ind. 46516

Magnamusic-Baton, Inc., 6390 Delmar Blvd., St. Louis, Mo. 63130

Manhassett Specialty Co., P.O. Box 2518, Yakima, Washington 98902

Melody Cradle Company, 1502 South Twelfth Street, Goshen, Indiana 46526

Mitchell Manufacturing Co., 2740 South 34th Street, Milwaukee, Wisconsin 53246

Pacific Music Papers, 1309 No. Highland Avenue, Hollywood, California 90028

Pacific Music Supply Co., 1143 Santee Street, Los Angeles, Calif. 90015

Peripole Products, Inc., 51-17 Rockaway Beach Blvd., Rockaway, L. I., N.Y. 11691

B. Portnoy Clarinet Accessories, 1715 Circle Drive, Bloomington, Indiana 47401

Rabco "ReeDuAl," Inc., P.O. Box 782, North Miami, Fla. 33161

Remo, Inc., 12804 Raymer Street, North Hollywood, Calif. 91605

Rhythm Band, Incorporated, P.O. Box 126, Fort Worth, Texas 76101

Rico Corporation, Box 3266, N. Hollywood, Calif. 91609

Oscar Schmidt-International, Inc., Garden State Road, Union, N. J. 07083

School Specialties, 48 W. Northfield Rd., Livingston, N. J. 07039

Schulmerich Carillons, Inc., Carillon Hill, Sellersville, Pa. 18960

Trophy Music Company, Div. of Grossman Music Corp., 1278 West 9th Street, Cleveland, Ohio 44113

Wenger Corporation, 555 Park Drive, Owatonna, Minn. 55060

PIANO AND ORGAN MANUFACTURERS

Baldwin Piano & Organ Company, 1801 Gilbert Avenue, Cincinnati, Ohio 45202

Conn Organ Corp., 1101 East Beardsley, Elkhart, Ind. 46514 Deerfield, Mass. 01373

Hammond Organ Company, 4200 West Diversey Avenue, Chicago, Illinois 60639

M. Hohner, Inc., Andrews Road, Hicksville, L. I., N.Y. 11802

Lowrey Organ & Piano Company, 7373 N. Cicero Avenue, Lincolnwood, Illinois 60646

Steinway & Sons, Steinway Place, Long Island City, N.Y. 11105

Story & Clark Piano Co., 7373 N. Cicero Avenue, Lincolnwood, Ill. 60646

The Wurlitzer Company, Wenger Corp., 555 Park Dr., Owatonna, Minn. 55060

Yamaha Musical Products, 3050 Breton Rd. N. E., Grand Rapids, Mich. 49510

COMPUTER ASSISTED INSTRUCTION

Micro-Music, Inc., 1535–121st Ave. S.E. Bellevue, Washington 98005

appendix E.
musical activities related to the treatment of mobility, endurance, and coordination problems

JOINT AND RELATED MUSCLE GROUPS

SPECIFIC MUSIC THERAPY ACTIVITY

1. NECK

Flexors (move head forward)

Piano and other Keyboard Instruments (high seating arrangement)
Mallett Instruments
    Marimba (high seating arrangement)
    Vibraharp (high seating arrangement)

Extensors (move head back)

Singing
Woodwind Instruments
Brass Instruments

Lateral Flexors (move head to side)

String Instruments
    Violin
    Viola

2. TRUNK
Flexor

String Instruments
    Cello
    Bass Viol
Percussion Instruments
    Tympani
    Bass drum

3. HIP

Flexors (move thigh up)

Keyboard and Harp Instruments
    Piano—pedalling (high seating arrangement at first; gradually lower)
    Organ—pedalling (high seating arrangement at first; gradually lower)
    Harp--pedalling (high seating arrangement at first; gradually lower)

This muscle chart is based on the "Muscle Examination Chart" of the National Foundation for Infantile Paralysis. The basis for the listing on dental formations is from the work of Dr. Howard E. Kessler, "Dental Changes produced by the Playing of Musical Wind Instruments," *Dental Survey,* Jan., 1956. Many of the musical acivities in this may be adapted for use in increasing endurance and strength of muscle groups. For example, certain instruments (or parts of instruments) may be redesigned in heavier materials so that greater activity becomes strongly resistive.

Extensors (move thigh down)

Keyboard Instruments
Piano—pedalling, tight-action pedal as resistance against gravity (low seating arrangement at first; gradually higher)
Organ—pedalling (low seating arrangement at first; gradually higher)

4. KNEE

Flexors (inner and outer ham-string muscles)

Keyboard Instruments
Piano—pedalling (best when hip is well flexed; high seating arrangement at first; gradually lower)

Extensors

Keyboard Instruments
Piano—pedalling; tight-action pedal as resistance against gravity (low seating arrangement at first; gradually higher)

5. ANKLE

Plantar-flexors (Gastroc and Soeleus—Ball of foot down when knee is extended)

Keyboard Instruments
Piano—pedalling (best when knee is held in extension in moderately high seating position)
Organ—swell pedal
Player Piano—treadling
Percussion Instruments
Bass Drum—pedal mechanism (also available are foot volume and tone controls)
Maracas—pedal operated

6. FOOT

Invertors (Anterior and Posterior Tilvialis)

Keyboard and Harp Instruments
Piano—pedalling (foot inverted)
Harp—pedalling (foot inverted)

Evertors (Peroneus Brevis and Longus)

Keyboard and Harp Instruments
Piano—pedalling (foot inverted)
Harp—pedalling (foot inverted)
Percussion Instruments
Bass Drum (foot volume and tone controls)
Maracas—pedal operated (foot everted)

7. SCAPULA (shoulder blade)

Abductor (Serratus Anterior)

Keyboard and Harp Instruments
Piano (cross-hand passage work)
Harp
Accordion
Concertina
String Instruments
Cello
Bass Viol
Mallet Played Instruments
Marimba (cross-hand passage work or the equivalent)

Adductors (Middle Trapezius and Rhomboids—move shoulder blades toward each other)	Keyboard and Harp Instruments
	    Piano (move four middle register to extreme registers of keyboard bilaterally)
	    Harp
	    Accordion
	    Concertina
	String Instruments
	    Cello
	    Bass Viol
	Woodwind Instruments
	    Saxophone
	    Bassoon

Elevators	Keyboard Instruments
	    Accordion
	    Concertina
	String Instruments
	    Violin
	    Viol
	Woodwind Instruments
	    Bassoon
	Brass Instruments
	    Trombone

Stabilizing Function	Any instrument which can be placed up high in order to bring the scapular muscles into a position of strongest stabilization.

8. SHOULDER

Flexors (arm forward at shoulder joint)	Mallet Played Instruments
	    Marimba
	    Vibraharp
	Percussion Instruments
	    Drums (use heavy drumsticks to counteract pull of gravity)
	Baton—conducting

Abductors (arm up and out to side)	Keyboard Instruments
	    Accordion
	Mallet Played Instruments
	    Vertical Chimes (place patient so that he stands with affected side toward chimes)

Horizontal Abductor	Keyboard Instruments
	    Accordion
	    Piano (use music containing scale and/or arpeggio passage work, or chords which move from middle register to extreme registers of keyboard)
	String Instruments
	    Violin
	    Viola
	    Cello
	Percussion Instruments
	    Cymbals

Horizontal Adductor

Keyboard Instruments
   Piano (use music containing scale and/or arpeggio passage work, or chords which move from extreme registers of keyboard to middle register)
   Accordion
   Concertina
String Instruments
   Violin
   Viola
   Cello
Mallett Played Instruments
Vibraharp
Baton—conducting

External Rotators

Toy Instruments
Percussion Instruments
   Melody Bells
Keyboard Instruments
   Piano—glissando passages with thumb

Internal Rotators

Toy Instruments
Percussion Instruments
Keyboard Instruments

9. ELBOW

Flexors

Plectrum Instruments
   Autoharp
   Guitar
   Banjo
   Mandolin
String Instruments
   Violin
   Viola
   Cello
Woodwind Instruments
   Clarinet
   Oboe
   English Horn
Keyboard and Harp Instruments
   Piano (slow playing, with emphasis on contraction and immediate relaxation of the biceps with some shoulder depression by triceps. Good for muscle strengthening at that joint—not for range of motion. Grade by means of gradually increasing volume of tone patient produces)
   Accordion
   Concertina
   Harp
Brass Instruments
   Trombone
Percussion Instruments
   Cymbals
   Sand Blocks
   Rhythm Sticks

Extensors

Autoharp
Guitar
Ukulele
Banjo
String Instruments
  Violin
  Viola
  Cello
  Bass Viol
Woodwind Instruments
  Clarnets
  Oboe
  English Horn
Keyboard and Harp Instruments
  Accordion
  Concertina
Brass Instruments
  Trombone
Percussion Instruments
  Rhythm Sticks
  Tambourine

10. FOREARM

Supinators (rotate forearm to turn palm up)

Keyboard Instruments
  Piano (use music containing arpeggios in contrary motion, broken in each hand from the thumb toward the fifth finger)
  Organ (dials)
  Accordion (buttons and bellows)
Percussion Instruments
  Tambourine
  Dumbbell Maracas
Plectrum Instruments
  Autoharp
  Guitar
  Banjo
  Mandolin

Pronators (rotate forearm to turn palm down)

Keyboard Instruments
  Piano (use music containing arpeggios in contrary motion)
  Organ (dials)
  Accordion (bellows)
Percussion Instruments
Plectrum Instruments

11. WRIST

Flexor (with radial deviation toward thumb of hand or with ulnar deviation toward 5th finger side of hand)

Plectrum Instruments
Keyboard Instruments
Brass Instruments
  Trumpet (manipulating a mute device)
Percussion Instruments

Extensors (with radial deviation toward thumb side of hand or with ulnar deviation toward 5th finger of hand)

Plectrum Instruments
Brass Instruments
  Trumpet (valves)
Woodwind Instruments
Percussion Instruments
  Triangle
  Bongo Drums (no sticks)
Keyboard Instruments

12. FINGERS

Flexors (metacarpophalangeal—bend at joint nearest wrist; known as MP joints)

Keyboard Instruments
    Piano (legato passage work)
Brass Instruments
Plectrum Instruments
Percussion Instruments
Woodwind Instruments

Extensors (metacarpophalangeal; MP joints)

Plectrum Instruments
    Autoharp (pressing bars)
    Guitar
    Banjo
Keyboard and Harp Instruments
    Piano (octave and large cord work)
    Chord Organ (pressing buttons with left hand; keys on manual with right hand)
    Harp
Woodwind Instruments
    Clarinet
    Oboe
    Saxophone
Percussion Instruments

Flexors (proximal interphalangeal—bend at joint second from wrist; known as IP joints)

Plectrum Instruments
Woodwind Instruments
    Recorder (stabilize MP joints)
Brass Instruments
    Clarinet (stabilize MP joints)
Keyboard and Harp Instruments
    Piano (sliding grace-note game or piece in which each finger slides from black key to adjacent white key. May stabliize MP joint by having palm of hand rest on wood rim under keyboard.)
    Organ
    Harp

Flexors (distal interphalangeal—bend at joint third from wrist; IP joints)

Plectrum Instruments
Woodwind Instruments
Brass Instruments
Keyboard and Harp Instruments
    Piano (see exercise above)

Abductors (spread fingers apart)

Keyboard and Harp Instruments
    Piano (wide chord work; or legato passages involving large stretches between fingers)
    Accordion
    Harp
    Organ
Woodwind Instruments
    Recorder (vertical flute)
    Clarinet
    Oboe
Percussion Instruments
    Castanets
    Finger Cymbals
Plectrum Instruments
    Guitar
    Ukulele
    Banjo

Adductors

Keyboard and Harp Instruments
Piano (passages in which thumb holds note, and other fingers move in toward it note-by-note)
Organ
Harp
Percussion Instruments
Plectrum Instruments

Opponens (5th finger rotates inward to touch thumb)

Keyboard Instruments
Piano (passage work in which thumb holds note and 5th finger moves in to play adjacent notes)
Percussion Instruments
Finger Cymbals (attached to thumb and to 5th finger; keep thumb stationary)

13. GROSS GRASP WITH FINGERS AND THUMB

Toy Instruments (Miniature animals which are activated to play the instruments they hold by means of a squeeze bulb attached to a rubber tube fastened to the animal, e.g., a monkey with cymbals, monkey with a drum, elephant with drum and cymbals.

14. THUMB
Opponens (thumb moves to touch any of the other fingers with an upwardly rotating motion)

Keyboard Instruments
Piano (passage work in which 5th finger holds note and thumb moves in to play adjacent of melody)
Organ
Percussion Instruments

Flexor (metacarpophalangeal—bend at joint nearest wrist)

Keyboard Instruments
Piano

15. FACIAL MUSCLES

Singing (relaxed "ah" vocalizing with lullaby or similarly soothing music)
Wind Instruments

16. PALATAL MUSCLES

Singing (relaxed "ah" vocalizing with lullaby or similarly soothing music)

17. LARYNGEAL MUSCLES

Singing (Vocalized sighs resulting in an "a" hum; humming to soothing appealing music)
Wind Instruments

18. RESPIRATORY MUSCLES AND LUNGS

Diaphragm (emphasis should be on maximum increase of diaphragmatic rather than intercostal breathing)

Wind Instruments
Rhythmic Breathing (to musical jingles, with music so adjusted that expiration phase is longer than inspiration phase. Upper portion of thorax should be kept as immobile as possible in order to increase "abdominal breathing")
Singing (diaphragmatic action)

19. MOUTH AND DENTAL FORMATIONS

Class II Type of Malocclusion

Brass Instruments
    Trumpets
    Cornet
    Bugle
    Tuba
Woodwind Instruments
    Flute
    Piccolo
    Oboe
    Bassoon

Class III Type of Malocclusion

Woodwind Instruments
    Clarinet
    Saxophone
    Bassoon

appendix F.
lists of songs for group singing

BROTHERHOOD

Born Free
Dona Nobis Pacem
Faith of Our Fathers
God of Our Fathers
He's Got the Whole World In His Hands
It's a Small, Small World
Kum Ba Yah, My Lord
Lift Every Voice and Sing

Let There Be Peace on Earth
Michael Row Your Boat
This Land Is Your Land
Vive L'Amour
What the World Needs Now
Let Us Break Bread Together
We Shall Overcome
Shalom Haverim

CAMPFIRE

Abide With Me
All Night All Day
All Through the Night
Aura Lee
Billy Boy
Deep River
Down in the Valley
Goodbye Old Paint
Good Night Ladies
Hey Ho Nobody
Home on the Range
In the Evening by the Moonlight
Jacob's` Ladder
Kum Ba Yah, My Lord

Lone Prairies
My Bonnie Lies Over the Ocean
Now the Day Is Over
Oh Dear, What Can the Matter Be?
Old Texas
On Top of Old Smoky
Red River Valley
She'll Be Comin' Round the Mountain
So Long
Streets of Laredo
Sweet and Low
Taps (Day Is Done)
Tell Me Why
There's a Long, Long Trail

COMBINED SONGS

(These songs, when sung smultaneously, can
provide a satisfying experience with harmony)
Are You Sleeping–Farmer in the Dell
A Spanish Cavalier–Solomon Levi
Keep the Home Fires Burning–Long, Long Trail
Lazy Mary Will You Get Up–London Bridge
Lone Star Trail–Old Texas
Mary Had a Little Lamb–Oh, Dear, What Can
the Matter Be?

My Home's in Montana–Home on the Range
Ring, Ring the Banjo–The Girl I Left Behind Me
Rock-a-My Soul–Ten Little Indians
Row Row Row Your Boat–Three Blind Mice
Sweetly Sings the Donkey–Where Is John?
Swing Low — All Through the Night

FUN AND NONSENSE

Bicycle Built for Two
Bingo
Blue Tail Fly
Boola-Boola
Camptown Races
Chumbara
Clementine
Deep in the Heart of Texas
Did You Ever See a Lassie?
Dinah
Do-Re-Mi
Down by the Station
Five Foot Two
For He's a Jolly Good Fellow
Hole in the Bucket
How Do You "Mr. ...."
If You're Happy and You Know It
I'm a Yankee Doodle Dandy
It Ain't Gonna Rain No More
John Jacob Jinkle Heimer Schmidt
La Cucuracha
Lazy Mary Will You Get Up

Li'l Liza Jane
My Bonnie Lie Over the Ocean
Oh Susannah
Oh Where, Oh Where Has My Little Dog Gone?
Old King Cole
Old MacDonald Had a Farm
Paper of Pins
Raindrops Keep Falling on My Head
Reuben & Rachel
Sarasponda
Shoo Fly
Skip to My Lou
Ta-Ra-Ra-Boom-de-ay
Ten Little Indians
The Keeper
The More We Get Together
There's a Tavern in the Town
This Old Man
While Strolling Through the Park One Day
Whistle a Happy Tune
Zulu Warrior

HERITAGE SONGS

Blow the Man Down
Carry Me Back to Old Virginny
Casey Jones
Clementine
Dixie
East Side, West Side
Erie Canal
God Bless America
God of Our Fathers
I've Been Workin' on the Railroad

Oh Susannah
Old Folks at Home
Red River Valley
Shenandoah
Streets of Laredo
Sweet Betsy from Pike
Swing Low, Sweet Chariot
This Is My Country
Yankee Doodle

HIKING

Across the Plain
A-Hunting We Will Go
Air Force Song
Anchors Aweigh
Battle Hymn of the Republic
Deep in the Heart of Texas
Don't Fence Me In
I've Been Working on the Raiload
I've Got Sixpence
Loch Lomond
Marching Along Together
Marching to Pretoria
Marines' Hymn
Oh Susannah
Onward Christian Soldiers

Sailing, Sailing
Stout Hearted Men
The Army Goes Rolling Along
The Campbells Are Coming
The Happy Wanderer
The Upward Trail
Vive L'Amour
Walking at Night
Waltzing Matilda
When Johnny Comes Marching Home Again
When the Saints Go Marching In
Yankee Doodle
You're a Grand Old Flag
Zum Gali Gali

HOLIDAY SONGS

Angels We Have Heard on High
Away in a Manger
Bring a Torch Jeanette Isabella
Come Ye Thankful People Come
Easter Parade
Greensleeves
Happy Birthday to You
I'm Dreaming of a White Christmas
Jingle Bells
Joy to the World

O Come All Ye Faithful
O Little Town of Bethlehem
Over the River and Through the Woods
Prayer of Thanksgiving
Silent Night
The First Noel
Up on the Housetop
We Three Kings
We Wish You a Merry Christmas

RELIGIOUS

All Night All Day
Deep River
Do Lord
Dona Nobis Pacem
Doxology
Everytime I Feel the Spirit
Fairest Lord Jesus
For the Beauty of the Earth
Go Down Moses
Golden Slippers
He's Got the Whole World in His Hands
I'm Goin' to Sing When the Spirit Says sing

Jacob's Ladder
Joshua Fought the Battle of Jericho
Kum Ba Yah, My Lord
Michael Row Your Boat
Nobody Knows the Trouble I've Seen
Old Hundred
Prayer of Thanksgiving
Rock of Ages
Steal Away
Swing Low Sweet Chariot
Were You There?
When Jesus Wept

ROUNDS

Alouette
Dona Nobis Pacem
For Health and Strength
French Cathedral Bell Round
Hey Ho Nobody Home
Kookaburra
Little Tom Tinker
Make New Friends

Music Alone Shall Live
Oh How Lovely Is the Evening
Scotland's Burning
Shalom Chaverim
Streets of Laredo
Sweetly Sings the Donkey
White Coral Bells

SENTIMENTAL

After the Ball Is Over
All Through the Night
Aloha 'Oe
Ashgrove
Auld Lang Syne
Believe Me If All Those Endearing Young Charms
Bells of St. Mary
Carry Me Back to Old Virginny
Cielito Lindo
Dear Hearts and Gentle People
Down by the Old Mill Stream
Down in the Valley
Drink to Me Only with Thine Eyes
Five Hundred Miles
Flow Gently Sweet Afton
Goodbye Old Paint

Keep the Home Fires Burning
Let Me Call You Sweetheart
Little Mohee
Long, Long Ago
Oh What a Beautiful Morning
Old Folks at Home
Red River Valley
Santa Lucia
Shenandoah
Sing Your Way Home
So Long
Sweet and Low
Tell Me Why
There's a Long, Long Trail
Wait Till the Sun Shines Nellie
Where Have All the Flowers Gone

song index